AGONIZING DECISION

"Carol, they say if you're going to give your baby up, you shouldn't ever see it. I mean you oughtn't to look even to see if it's a boy or girl. If you don't really see it, it's easier not to keep it. That's what they said—don't look and it won't hurt.

"I don't know if I could keep from looking, Carol, unless I was unconscious or something."

She ran down then, and silence closed in. You could hear the clock ticking in the dining room and the wind in the trees.

In this tender, sympathetic and honest novel, a young girl searches for the mature wisdom needed to help her older sister make the most agonizing decision of her life.

Other Avon Books by
Richard Peck

AMANDA/MIRANDA
PICTURES THAT STORM INSIDE MY HEAD

DON'T LOOK AND IT WON'T HURT

RICHARD PECK

AN AVON  FLARE BOOK

The verse quoted in toto on pages 22-23 and in part on pages 140-141 is "Little Donkey Close Your Eyes" by Margaret Wise Brown; Reprinted from NIBBLE, NIBBLE, text © 1959 by Margaret Wise Brown, a Young Scott Book, by permission of Addison-Wesley Publishing Company.

The lines on page 63 are from "She's Leaving Home" by John Lennon and Paul McCartney. Copyright 1967 for the World Northern Songs Limited.

AVON BOOKS
A division of
The Hearst Corporation
959 Eighth Avenue
New York, New York 10019

Copyright © 1972 by Richard Peck.
Published by arrangement with Holt, Rinehart and Winston, Inc.
Library of Congress Catalog Card Number: 70-185053.
ISBN: 0-380-00781-9

First Avon Printing, October, 1973.
First Flare Printing, May, 1983.

FLARE TRADEMARK REG. U.S. PAT. OFF. AND
OTHER COUNTRIES, REGISTERED TRADEMARK—
MARCA REGISTRADA, HECHO EN U.S.A.

Printed in the U.S.A.

WFH   29   28   27   26   25   24   23   22   21

for Ingrid

DON'T LOOK
AND IT
WON'T HURT

1 | Out at the city limits, there's this sign that says: WELCOME TO CLAYPITTS, PEARL OF THE PRAIRIE and if you'd believe that, you'd believe anything. The truth is, it's the kind of town you drive right through without noticing. In fact, you drive around it on the Interstate and just keep going. Not a bad idea. What can you expect from a town called Claypitts? It's where we live, though. In the wrong end of it at that. And in half a house, which makes sense in a way because we're only sort of half a family: three not-exceptional daughters and one exasperated mother.

I don't know where you go from a town like Claypitts. I'm still trying to figure that out. There was a time when I thought the world began and ended right here. Believe me, this was no encouraging thought, considering we're not what you'd call Prominent Members of the Community.

But a few things that have happened lately have sort of raised my sights. I've lived all my fifteen and three-quarters years in Claypitts. In fact, I've almost never been out of town except for one trip up to Chicago. That's eight hours on the bus with stops and just under seven dollars each way, so normally it's quite a bit out of my range. But I had to go up there a while back to see my sister. I'd like to go again someday and really have a look around. The trip I made was more like a mission.

I went up to see Ellen. She's seventeen, going on twelve the way she acts sometimes. And my other sister's Liz. She's nine, but a kind of elderly nine—half little kid, half little old lady.

I'm Carol. Carol Patterson. The one in the middle.

I had to run off in the middle of the night to see Ellen. And so, I couldn't take Liz with me. I used to be very conscientious about looking after her, but not this time. Nobody likes being left behind, Liz included. On the other hand, she doesn't want anybody hovering over her day and night. She's independent. In a way, I really admire her. And how many nine-year-olds can you say that about?

Mom works at the restaurant out by the Interstate exit. It's called "The Pull-Off Plaza." (How's that for real class?) She's the hostess who goes crazy seating people when charter groups pile off buses and gang in there with maybe twenty minutes to eat.

If you've ever been in the place, you've probably seen her. She's the lady with the orangey hair and black dress holding the menus and saying, "How many, please?" All night.

But her hostess status is pretty important to her. When they really get rushed or shorthanded or something, though, she has to pitch in and help the waitresses hustle the grub. After nights like that, she comes home with this destroyed look on her face and sits in the living room with her feet in a pan of hot water.

One morning, I found her still sitting there, sound asleep. Sun streaming in the window, and there she was, completely out, in her girdle and her black dress and her bracelets, with her feet swollen and dead-white in the cold water. I started to wake her up. But I was beginning to cry. So I left her where I found her. And I cried all the way to school.

Being the one in the middle never seemed like much of a life to me. And I'm never going to win any popularity contests at school. Mom works the four-to-eleven shift, so I've always had to go straight home after school and keep an eye on Liz in the evenings. I'm not complaining. I have a friend or two I can count on, but when it comes to being In . . . I'm out.

With Ellen, it was always a different story. You'd never catch her speeding home from school to look after anybody. "I can depend on *you*," Mom always said to me. So I'd get the responsibility, and Ellen got the popularity . . . if that's what you want to call it.

The first friend I ever managed to have turned out to be a disaster. We were best buddies from the fourth grade up till seventh. Her name was Laurie Pence—it still is, not that it matters. We had this teacher in fourth who had a passion for the alphabet. Patterson was seated just in front of Pence, so we began this whispering friendship. And recess. We were still in the hula hoop–Yo-Yo stage, and I thought Laurie was the greatest. Everything she did was okay by me.

She wasn't as good as I was in school, but what does that matter in fourth grade? She was everything I wanted to be, including popular, and she'd chosen me for a friend! Remem-

11

ber, I warned you. This relationship was headed for disaster.

One day, she invited me to her house for lunch on a Saturday. This meant we were more than school friends, and I was delirious with joy.

The Pences live in a neighborhood called Montgomery Place, pure class, Claypitts style. I don't know what my grade-school mind was expecting—white pillars and a fountain and a curving drive with a Cadillac or something like that. But it was different, more impressive in a way. They did have a Cadillac, incidentally, but the house was sort of plain and quiet. Everything one color. Pale beige carpeting everywhere and the same color on the walls. And a little lunch table with a skirt on it all set up for just Laurie and me, with water goblets up on very fragile stems and heavy, beige linen napkins.

Laurie showed me her room afterwards. She had a million toys and enough clothes to stock a store, but everything had its place behind sliding doors. I think they hired a woman just to patrol the house, picking up everything and putting it out of sight. And Laurie had a bed with a little, snowy-white canopy over it. That's what knocked me out. I stood there and looked at it like somebody they'd checked out of an orphanage for the day.

The Pences are what Mom calls "country club people," not in a sneering way, but just like they're foreigners or Martians or something out of our world, which they are. Laurie's mother is a cool champagne blonde, or was at the time. She tended to melt into the rooms of that house like you had to look around to find her. And then there she was, with this beautiful face and hardly any lipstick. She gave me the discreet third degree, asking a lot about school and nothing about home. Laurie had probably told her I wasn't from one of the Beautiful People families. Come to think of it, she could probably figure that out for herself. She couldn't help but notice I was gawking at that house like I'd died and gone to heaven.

She started telling me how interior decoration was her big passion, and how she'd worked for a store in St. Louis before she married Mr. Pence. She even put forth some of her theories about the way houses should look and used phrases like "gracious living" and "simplicity is the keynote" and like that. I hadn't ever heard such talk in my life, and I was goggle-eyed. Mrs. Pence was talking to me like I was grownup or nearly. Then we both noticed that Laurie wasn't too happy about this. She was beginning to stalk around the room. Laurie doesn't have much of an attention span anyway.

And that's about all there was to my one and only brush with Claypitts High Society. Though we stayed friends for three years after that, Laurie never invited me home again. Probably because I never returned her invitation. How could I?

I remember when I came home from the Pences that day, I looked around our place and nearly got sick. Our half of the old frame house has a narrow little living room you can nearly reach across. And talk about clutter. I went straight down to the basement and lugged back a big cardboard box and started throwing stuff into it. Anything loose in the living room went into that box: all the cracked ash trays put out for company we never have, and an awful two-color, frilly doily starched to stand up in revolting curlicues, and the loose covers to protect the arms on the old collapsed sofa, and everything off the mantel and the top of the radiator. I'd have had the pictures down off the walls if I could have reached them.

When the box was about full, I stopped and looked around the room. Then I really was sick. It was the junk in the box that had made the room bearable. Without it, the place looked ten times worse. The wallpaper just above the mantel was curling out and hanging in shreds. Stuffing showed through on the sofa arms. The coffee table top was warped. I saw all this through a blur. But I saw it. Then Mom walked in.

She just stood there, looking astounded. She saw the box. Then she looked at me. And because something had to fill up the awful silence, I said, "Simplicity is the keynote."

She came over and got down on her knees in front of me and took me by the arms, very gently, and made me look at her. "Honey, I know where you got that, and it just won't work here."

She got up and walked out of the room then and stayed out until I had everything out of the box and back in its place.

But like I say, this didn't wreck my friendship with Miss Laurie Pence in her beige-carpeted cocoon. It was a little incident in seventh-grade English. We were in our first year in the

14

junior high building. The homework gets a little heavier that year, and I'm okay there because I'm home in plenty of time to get it done. Laurie wasn't doing so well. Or like they say in the Guidance Office, she wasn't making a very "satisfactory transition."

Our first-semester English teacher was Mr. Mifflin. We called him "The Muffin," and everybody loved him. He was young and skinny and wore very wide ties. He wasn't what you'd call a very demanding teacher. We had quite a lot of conversation and very little work, and everyone concerned was happy with the arrangement.

Then tragedy struck. The Muffin got drafted. We couldn't believe it at first. But we talked it all over in class, and The Muffin explained to us that his draft board wasn't allowing any more teaching deferments. Then he tried to explain how the system works, how some men get deferments and others don't, and how it's not a very fair system, but that's the way it is. We must have talked about it for a week's worth of classes. Some of us were all for writing a letter of protest to the newspaper or staging a sit-in at the draft board. But he said, no, he'd go and get it over with. So, on his last day, we gave him a big party and a shaving kit to take to Fort Leonard Wood, where he was going for Basic Training. Just before the bell rang, he picked up the shaving kit, tucked it under his arm, and started out of the room. At the door he turned around, gave us the peace sign, and then he was gone. Talk about a depressed bunch of kids.

Well, The Muffin was Our Hero and a tough

act to follow. His replacement for second semester was a Miss Olmquist. And to be fair, she didn't stand a chance. She was young, too, right out of college, I think. And full of constructive ideas. But every time she tried something new, somebody would pipe up, "We never did that with Mr. Mifflin," or words to that effect. Usually, that somebody was Laurie. Miss Olmquist wasn't too easily discouraged, though. And she really wanted us to learn. To put it in a nutshell, she wanted to be our teacher, and we wanted our buddy back. With a situation like this, it's all downhill.

One time after we'd read *The Call of the Wild*, Miss Olmquist asked us to write a paper describing what we thought was good or bad about it. "Be specific," she said, and then wrote it in big letters on the board:

BE SPECIFIC.

I heard this bored little sigh coming from Laurie sitting behind me. She hadn't even read *The Call of the Wild*. She hasn't read anything since Little Golden Books. Then she started poking me in the back. I kept writing and didn't turn around, so pretty soon Laurie started talking to one of her other "friends" across the aisle. It was Susan Steadman, a born follower. So Laurie and Susan started up this long conversation that kept getting louder.

Finally, Miss Olmquist said, "Laurie, Susan, get to work please; you only have forty minutes." Did this stop Laurie? She never looked up. She just kept on talking to Susan who would go along with anything. Then Miss Olmquist stood up at her desk and said, "I'm sure what you two are discussing isn't as important as writing your papers."

And then came Laurie's reply: "Don't be too sure."

"What did you say?" Miss Olmquist asked in this I'm-trying-to-stay-calm voice.

"I said, anything is more important than this stupid paper." Laurie looked around the room as if she expected the rest of us to wad up our papers and throw them at Miss Olmquist in unison. But we all sat there, stunned.

"Leave the room," Miss Olmquist said, while everybody turned and looked at Laurie. "Take your books and leave the room, I said!" Her voice cracked a little and jumped up at the end. I don't know what Laurie was expecting from her, but I think this came as a surprise, which shows you how dumb Laurie is.

Finally, she got up and slowly headed for the door. But it wouldn't be like Laurie to leave without an exit line. At the door, she turned and looked straight at Miss Olmquist and said, "And just where am I supposed to go?"

That was Miss Olmquist's cue to fire back, "To the Principal's Office!" but she fumbled it. There was a second of hesitation. Instead, she said, "Out in the hall."

After the rest of us got reasonably quiet, Miss Olmquist followed Laurie out of the room. When the bell rang and we changed classes, they were still out there. Miss Olmquist was talking very earnestly, and Laurie was lounging against the wall, looking around very bored.

Unfortunately, our lockers were right next to each other. After school that day, I was grabbing my books and Ellen's hand-me-down win-

17

ter coat and trying to make a quick getaway. But Laurie strutted up looking like she'd just won World War III. I wasn't going to say anything, but she wasn't about to let me get away with that. "Well," she said, very nonchalant, "what did you think of English today?" What I thought was that I'd like to mind my own business and let Laurie mind hers.

But something made me say, "I think you got off pretty easy not being sent down to the principal." Now that wasn't even close to what Laurie wanted to hear, but it was an answer she could deal with.

"You aren't stupid enough to think Olmquist would send me to the principal, are you? Come on! She's a new teacher. Do you honestly think she'd want the principal to find out she can't handle her classes?" The only thing I wanted from this conversation was *out*, so I just gave a little shrug and closed my locker door.

By this time, a few of Laurie's more ardent followers were gathering around, male and female, led by the ever-faithful Susan. Laurie had drawn a good crowd, and she wanted some kind of satisfactory rise out of me. "Besides, you're forgetting one other little point, Carol. My father's on the school board. I can make Olmquist wish *she'd* been drafted!"

This thrilling speech brought a round of cheers and applause. Seventh-grade English class had lost their hero, but they'd found their heroine. And there I was in the middle again. "That's fine, Laurie, that's just great," I muttered and started to leave.

But, of course, I didn't get off that easy. In a voice designed to enlarge the crowd, Laurie

18

yelled out, "Well, it looks like Olmquist has *one* friend—Miss Last-Year's-Coat Carol Patterson!"

I just walked away then. In a way, I've done a lot of walking away ever since.

2 | So much for my Zero Social Status. I managed to adjust to it, more or less, but the rest of seventh grade was a mild form of Eternal Damnation. It doesn't take much to sour you at that age. So it figured that when summer came, and I was high and dry, I sort of took Liz over. Before that, Mom had to twist my arm whenever Liz needed taking care of, but by then, I was pretty desperate for some human contact. Ellen was out of the question, so it was Liz.

She was an independent little character even then. And she could take care of herself pretty well. I mean you didn't have to worry about her falling off the roof or playing in the traffic. To tell you the truth, she could get along without me fine. I was the one who needed her.

She was kind of a worrier, though, even then. We couldn't afford a TV so she's probably the last human child on the face of the earth to grow up without The Tube. She liked books, even before she could read them. She was going to start first grade that fall and was worried because she couldn't read. Somehow, Liz got the idea you were supposed to be able to read *before* you start school. Otherwise, they wouldn't be able to teach you anything. I never could quite convince her that it was the school's job to teach you how to read.

She had the notion that if I read to her and

she looked at the pictures, sooner or later, she could put the two together and she'd be reading. So, we went to the library a lot that summer. I guess we checked out every book in the children's section. At night, she'd sit next to me with her head on my arm, looking very solemn and trying to stay awake. She wasn't enjoying it much. It was just something she thought she ought to do. And she'd get very nervous if we came to a page with writing and no pictures.

Poetry was different, though. She felt it in a way and didn't worry if there wasn't a picture to go with it. Come to think of it, there was just one poem she was that way about, and I guess it was because she had it memorized. We both did. Finally, I could say one stanza, and she'd answer with the next. Even now, I still know it:

> Little Donkey on the hill
> Standing there so very still
> Making faces at the skies
> Little Donkey close your eyes.
>
> Little Monkey in the tree
> Swinging there so merrily
> Throwing coconuts at the skies
> Little Monkey close your eyes.
>
> Silly Sheep that slowly crop
> Night has come and you must stop
> Chewing grass beneath the skies
> Silly Sheep now close your eyes.
>
> Little Pig that squeals about
> Make no noises with your snout
> No more squealing to the skies
> Little Pig now close your eyes.

Wild Young Birds that sweetly sing
Curve your heads beneath your wing
Dark night covers all the skies
Wild Young Birds now close your eyes.

Old Black Cat down in the barn
Keeping five small kittens warm
Let the wind blow in the skies
Dear Old Black Cat close your eyes.

Little Child all tucked in bed
Looking such a sleepy head
Stars are quiet in the skies
Little Child now close your eyes.

That last stanza was always mine. By then, old Liz was usually groggy and half asleep, and the reading lesson for the night was over. Just the other day when I asked her if she remembered that poem, she drew a complete blank. So I started rattling it off: "Little Donkey on the hill—" I could have quoted the whole thing letter-perfect, but she gave me this strange look like I was beginning to rave. So much for memories. That's another one I'm stuck with alone.

We went to the park a lot that summer, too. There are only two parks in town. The really nice one up by Montgomery Place and the ratty looking one nearer our house. It's not what you'd call much of a park—a square block of flat ground and some swings. Kind of a glorified vacant lot.

But I was giving the Montgomery Place neighborhood a wide berth in those days just in case Laurie and Her Socialites might be out taking a breath of air. There wasn't much to do in our park. We'd look for birds' nests, which we never found, and see how close we could get to squirrels. Sometimes, we'd take peanut butter sandwiches and sit there in the middle of the park in the blazing sun, having a picnic. It was better than nothing.

All those park days were pretty much alike except one. We'd been to the library that morning, so we had our usual quota of kiddies' books. We were sitting on the swings. I was reading a Dr. Seuss to Liz, and she was leaning over, straining to see the pictures. I don't know why, but pretty soon I noticed that this old wreck of a truck was driving around the park. It must have gone around three or four times, slow. Then it stopped, and a man got out. He was a big heavy-set guy wearing a battered ball cap, which he took off while he wiped the sweat off his forehead. A mongrel dog jumped out of the bed of the truck and started sniffing around the grass. While this old guy was looking at us, it dawned on me that we were the only people in the park. Who else would be out on a day that hot without a tree in sight?

Well, you know how mothers are always telling you not to have anything to do with strange men in parks. We've all heard it. I even considered snatching up Liz and seeing how fast we could make it back to civilization. But I figured he could always set his dog on us, and it would be yapping at my ankles before we got halfway to the other street. So I just sat there pretending to be involved with Dr. Seuss. Just to make the moment complete, Liz slipped down out of the swing, said, "I'm going to play with that doggie," and was off before I could lay a hand on her.

What could I do? I started out after her, but she's quick. She and the dog met in the middle and started rolling around on the grass. At least, the dog was harmless. The man seemed okay, too. I began to think maybe he just stopped to let his dog have a run in the park, which is illegal, by the way. So I stopped running but kept my distance from him.

After a while, the whole scene was less scary, but sort of tense. The man and I watched Liz and the dog going crazy over each other. Finally, he said, "That little one your sister?" I nodded. "She ought to have her a puppy," he said. "Every kid ought to." I nodded again.

Finally, he started to go but then turned around and said, "Hot, ain't it?" I wasn't much for small talk in those days, but it wasn't really a question. He started fumbling in his pockets and pulled out a couple of quarters.

"Here you go. Take sis and get you something cool to drink." The Don't-Take-Money-from-Strangers bit is another old saw, and I think he remembered it himself. Especially since I was still keeping out of range.

"We got money," I said, which was a lie.

"Go on, I want you to have it." Then he bent down and put the quarters on the curb. While I was eying them, he swung himself up into the cab of the truck and banged the side of the door, which was his dog's signal to scramble back aboard.

I was relieved to see him ready to pull out. But he hesitated a moment like he had something else he wanted to say. Then he leaned out of the truck and yelled over, "What's the little one's name?"

I figured it was safe to tell him. Then he really gave me a shock. By saying, "Then you must be Carol."

I nodded, just as before, but he could tell I was caught offguard. The truck lurched away from the curb, with the mongrel dog barking and pretending to try to jump over the tailgate. Just as they pulled away, I saw a hand-lettered sign on the back bumper:

ROUTE 7 FIXIT SHOP

I waited till the truck was out of sight before I scooped up the quarters.

And I wouldn't have told anybody about it, but somehow, we didn't get those quarters spent that day. They were still rattling around in my pocket when we got home. Mom was fixing a cold supper for us before she went off to work, as usual. She has a sharp ear for loose change, probably because she has a nightly battle with the waitresses at The Pull-Off Plaza. They're supposed to divide up their tips evenly, but it isn't a smoothly running arrangement. Mom has the job of seeing that nobody holds out on anybody else.

She wanted to know where those quarters came from, and I wasn't too anxious to tell her. On the other hand, I didn't want her thinking I'd mugged a little old lady for them. So the story came out. I expected a routine warning about money from strangers, but she listened very carefully and looked strange. In fact, she looked mad—very mad. I kept talking to make a long story out of it, seeing as how she was

25

about to light into me. I thought maybe she'd cool off, but she didn't. When I told her the guy must have run a fix-it shop, she really let me have it.

"Come on, Carol, that man was no stranger to you, and you know it!"

Even while I was swearing I didn't know him, something told me I did. Something mostly forgotten, but there. Maybe I'd known all afternoon that he was my father.

But he was still a stranger to me, and he'd have kept right on being one if Mom hadn't forced me to face up to it. He walked out on us just after Liz was born. I was around six then, old enough to know him, to remember. But somehow I hadn't. Talk about him was a taboo around our house. Ellen, who was old enough to remember him better than I, had never mentioned his name. He was more completely gone than if he'd been dead. But I knew he wasn't. I knew he was alive. I guess maybe I even knew he'd never left Claypitts. But that had all happened half my lifetime ago. I'd had time to make up a dozen dream fathers who managed to crowd the real one out of my mind.

I'd never made myself remember the real one. But I could give you long and detailed descriptions of the dream ones—secret agents, uranium miners, amnesia victims, astronauts lost in space, successful engineers who return years later from building bridges in Bolivia to shower expensive presents on their waiting daughters— especially the middle one.

But never a workman in greasy coveralls who left quarters on the curb after six years of living out at the edge of town. Never.

While I was busy sorting through the fantasies to get to the reality, Mom was still carrying on. Usually, she's too tired to get this mad. But now she was making an exception. "You've seen him before, haven't you? You've been seeing him right along, haven't you? Answer me!" She was getting loud, and I was trying to get away.

She had me by the arm, and she was going to shake an answer out of me. "No," I was screaming, "I never saw him before. I wish I never had seen him!" Then with my free hand, I reached into my pocket and pulled the money out. I threw it on the kitchen floor and yelled, "Take the damn quarters!" Then Mom slapped me across the mouth, hard.

I went down on the floor on my back, squalling and kicking like a kindergartner. I was more mad than hurt. But I was hurt in a way that had nothing to do with my stinging mouth. I guess I planned to thrash around on the floor until Mom came to her senses and realized she'd done me a great injustice. Instead, she said in her coldest voice: "I'm not through with you yet." And without another word, she left for work.

I decided to be in bed and sound asleep by the time Mom got home that night. Ellen and Liz and I have to share one poky little room. But Ellen was out, as usual, and Liz had been dead to the world for hours. I was waiting for Mom to come home so I could go into my sleeping act. I heard her come up the stairs. Maybe she'd go straight back to her room. But then the door opened very slowly. At that point, I was torn between being awake to hear her apologies and being asleep to let her suffer. As a compromise, I had one eye open and the other one shut. She stood at the door for a while. Her shadow was long on the floor.

Then she came over and sat down on my bed. "Okay, Carol, let's talk about it."

I've wished ever since that night that I'd thrown myself more wholeheartedly into a sleeping act. Instead, I said, "You hit me."

"I was mad," she said. "I thought you'd been lying to me."

"I wasn't lying. I don't lie."

She put her hand on my shoulder. "But you knew who it was. You must have."

"No, I didn't, I tell you. He left years ago. You never mention him. How was I supposed to know?"

She was quiet awhile, thinking this over, probably trying to see the situation from the viewpoint of a thirteen-year-old kid. Then she said with a shaky little sigh, "I guess it was bound to happen. I guess I was mad because I told your father never to come near any of you ever."

"What right did you have to do that?" I was pushing my luck now and didn't have sense enough to know it.

"I had every right." She didn't remind me then who'd raised us singlehandedly and worked the night shift to keep the well-known wolf from the door. I thought of that later.

Her quiet voice was beginning to rattle me. This wasn't the same woman who had been slapping me around the kitchen a few hours earlier. So, instead of a big kiss good-night and let's forget the whole mess, I had to push it one step more: "Why did he leave?"

She kind of pulled back at that. "You'll find out someday when you're ready to know."

"I'm ready now."

No response.

Then I sort of mumbled, "Maybe I know already. Maybe he was just tired of you."

Now, almost three years later, I'd like to have those words back. They didn't earn me another slap across the mouth. I wish they had. Mom walked out of the room, and life went on, not quite like before, but it went on. And after that, every time I saw an old wreck of an open-bed truck coming up the street, I'd duck down an alley.

3 | And there you have the thrilling saga of my pathetic puberty. I thought it would go creeping on forever, but things change, even in my life. Let's see now, when did it all start to happen?

I guess it began in Women's Prison. That's what I used to call the bedroom Ellen, Liz, and I were forced to share. All that room needs is bars on the window to make the cell atmosphere complete. Ellen and I had twin beds jammed together, and Liz slept in her junior cot wedged in at our feet.

The room was hardly big enough for one decent-sized bed, so it was wall-to-wall mattresses and a closet door you could only open halfway. If you knew Ellen, you'd know who got the privilege of sleeping next to the window to catch the occasional breath of fresh air.

I, of course, slept next to the door. So when Ellen wandered in at night, she took great delight in tramping all over my slumbering form on the way to her bed.

I guess that's about all I ever expected Ellen to be in my life. A nightly series of heavy footsteps in the small of my back. I don't know now if I ever envied Ellen her freedom at the time. I knew it wasn't just a matter of her being a couple of years older. I never really believed I'd just come and go as I pleased like she did.

She hadn't earned any of her freedom, or even fought for it. She had Mom over a barrel. Short of calling out the Juvenile Authorities, Mom had no control over her. She never came home from school until Mom left for work. And by the time Mom got in around midnight, Ellen was either still out or asleep. Talk about a communication gap. Compared to this, Mom and I were almost bosom buddies.

Not that I minded much—about Ellen's freedom, I mean. Maybe I just thought that's the way big sisters are—not really sisters at all. I didn't care much for myself, but, in a way, I did for Liz. At least Ellen would sort of grunt at me in the mornings—warn me not to borrow any of her stuff and things like that. But she ignored Liz completely, as if she didn't even exist. Liz didn't mind, of course. Little kids adjust to anything—or nothing. But I minded for her.

Then, one night last spring Ellen came home earlier than usual. Instead of staggering over me in the dark and flopping down in her bed, she switched on the overhead light.

"Wake up, Maewest," she said in a voice that brought me bolt upright. It even made old Liz toss around a little. Now I'd better explain that in the rare moments when Ellen addressed me, she called me "Maewest." In case you don't know, Mae West was this old-time movie star. She's famous for her large, well-developed bosom. I'm not. So this gives you an idea of the level of Ellen's humor. I won't dwell on this subject. It's possible that I'm just a late bloomer.

So I was awake, and wonder of wonders, Ellen sat down on my bed. Girl talk with Ellen? This was a Famous First. "Are you sure you're awake?" she asked, as if she was really interested.

"Who could sleep through that entrance? Are you sure you aren't in the wrong house or something?"

Then Ellen gave me this adult-style surprised look, just as if she and I were well-known for our little nightly chats. I decided to keep quiet and see what was on her mind. And while I was keeping still, I noticed something else new. Ellen was pretty. Maybe she'd just suddenly turned pretty that night, or maybe she'd been working toward prettiness all along. After all, I wouldn't have been the first to notice. But she just sat there on the bed and glowed. You couldn't help seeing it. Her hair, which is mousebrown like mine, had these auburn lights in it, and her eyes, not her best feature, were sparkling. I decided I must be seeing her for the first time.

And to be honest, I liked the idea of my big sister waking me up to confide in me. So I punched up my pillow and got comfortable. Down at the foot of the bed, Liz was wideawake now, sitting up ready to drink it all in, her eyes as big and rounds as, well—two quarters. Ellen never even noticed her.

But Ellen had a lot on her mind that night. And it all centered around a New Boy. She was saying things like "This is the Real Thing," and "He's so mature," and "Nothing like the creeps I've been running around with." It was all like that. Trust Ellen to label all her former boyfriends *creeps* the minute somebody better comes along. Creeps, however, does tend to describe them.

I've caught more glimpses of Ellen by strolling by McDonald's Hamburger Stand than I have around home. She was always smack in the center of a gang of high-school hotshots who all looked like they were on the verge of flunking Remedial Reading. There's nothing more scraggly than a cluster of small-town hippies, and Ellen had been queen of them all through her junior year.

I don't mean any of them went the whole hippie route. It was just sort of their In-image. It was about the only thing to be if you weren't in the Smart Set. Actually, they had enough trouble carrying off the hippie image since none of them had the money for all the suede and beadwork and like that. So they let it go with Levi jackets with cut off sleeves and long hair and the occasional Genuine Simulated Leather jacket.

In that crowd, there's a fine line between hippie and hood. Ellen managed to straddle it. But now, she'd met Mr. Wonderful, so it was goodbye to the Old Life.

She stopped to catch her breath, and I sat back waiting for a full technicolor description of him. I could just visualize the shoulder-length hair, tie-dyed tanktop, the thonged sandals, and the souped-up Mercury Cougar.

But on that momentous night, Ellen had turned into a mind reader. "I know what you're thinking, and you're wrong as usual. He's really mature. He's twenty."

This was designed to impress me, and frankly, it did. "Does he go to State?" I never pictured

Ellen in the same league with the local girls who date college boys.

"No," she said. "He saw through that college rat race. Left after his freshman year, back east. Lost his student deferment and everything. He's not a *talker*, you know. He's a *doer*."

I remembered The Muffin then, marching bravely off to the army, flashing the peace sign. It sounded to me like Ellen's Mr. Wonderful was about to turn into Private Wonderful of the Infantry.

"He's fighting it," Ellen went on. "The draft board I mean. It's part of what he believes in. Part of his work."

"What work?"

Then she got cagey. There was a Big Secret in here somewhere to add to the glamour of the new romance. But Ellen wasn't really ready to clam up. If I'd gone into a coma, it wouldn't have stopped her.

It turned out that his name was Kevin Coleman. A good, straight name, at any rate, and a refreshing change from the Butches, Dizzies, Ratsos, and Tigers whose names littered the cover of Ellen's grubby Secretarial Science notebook. But she stalled a little when I asked her where he was from.

"Oh, around."

"Around here?"

"Not really, but he's staying out at Mitsy Decker's cabin on the lake. She introduced us. That's sort of his base of operations right now. He's free to work from the cabin until the Deckers start going out in the summer."

I was growing a little weary of this cloak-and-dagger conversation. It was sheer nuttiness to

34

pump Ellen for information she was dying to tell me anyway. So when I stopped looking interested, she opened up, after swearing me to secrecy. We had to go through the cross-your-heart business and everything. This could only mean not telling Mom. As far as Ellen was concerned, we were alone in the room. She probably thought Liz was a stuffed panda propped up on the bed.

It turned out that Kevin's great mission was helping draft dodgers avoid the army by smuggling them out of the country. He was a sort of way station on the underground railroad. He'd been working in this territory all year, according to Ellen, but he was away a lot, conducting fugitives to the border, and helping them with money, and telling them how to get legal aid. According to her, Kevin was an important cog in a well-oiled machine of deeply committed people—which didn't sound like Ellen talking at all.

There's no telling how long this conversation might have gone on—probably till dawn's early light. And I enjoyed it. It didn't matter that Ellen talked as if she'd just invented draft resistance. It didn't even matter that she wasn't interested in hearing about The Muffin. What did matter was that we were actually talking, even if it was one-sided. Then we heard Mom coming in at the kitchen door. So it was lights out.

I was dumb enough to expect a nightly continuation of the new sisterhood, but we lapsed back into the old routine. Oh, occasionally Ellen would give me a wink and a nod in passing that said we've-got-a-wonderful-secret. And being in love improved her disposition somewhat. She was even home earlier than Mom usually. There were times when Kevin must have been away on Secret Business. Then, Ellen went around with a patiently suffering look. I think Mom sensed a change in the air, but it wasn't anything she could identify. Besides, everything was going smoothly, and that's about the best she could expect.

One night, I heard a car outside, so I scrambled ever onto Ellen's bed in time to see her walking with Kevin up to the front porch. Then, after a long interval, I watched him going back to his car alone. There was just time to catch a glimpse of him under the street light. Then, was I impressed! He was wearing a dark business suit—and he had short hair! Ellen was obviously into something new. In the time it took her to get upstairs, I was back in my own bed, sound asleep and snoring daintily.

4 | Those were the last days of the Old Life —and, like I say, they were fairly easy-going. Ellen floated in and out—mostly out—on a cloud of young love. She even managed to tidy up her appearance somewhat. At least she stopped wearing the plastic windbreaker that had BIG LOSERS, INCORPORATED lettered across the back. That garment had been a kind of symbol for her high position in the old gang. Apparently, she'd outgrown the tribe.

Liz was growing up, too. She could read on her own, of course, without benefit of pictures —or me. Mom stuck with the nightly grind. She fought the battle against varicose veins with elastic hose and kept her two regulation black dresses in working order.

And me? I was miscast against my will in the ninth-grade level of the College Prep program. Higher powers in the Guidance Office had me pegged for college because of my grades. Nothing could change their decision. As often as I explained that college was OUT OF THE QUESTION, they started carrying on about scholarships and loans. They don't seem to be able to grasp the idea of real poverty.

And since State University is a mere twenty miles down the Interstate, they figured it's within the reach of all. It might as well be on the moon, but nothing I could say mattered. In their

37

one-track minds, I was College Material. So I found myself in first-year Spanish, upper-level English, something odd called Contemporary World Problems, and algebra. This put me in with a brand new group of nonfriends, so I was learning to be a social outcast all over again.

And it was a lot more work, leading to exactly nothing. On the other hand, I had nothing better to do at the time. Besides, Spanish was mostly memorizing. And there was always Contemporary World Problems to brighten the day.

Our teacher for this class was one Mr. Peterson. An individual with a bulbous thinker's brow, who wore slept-in seersucker suits. Mr. Peterson's idea of a contemporary world problem was the Second World War. Probably because he'd been in it. It always seemed to agitate him that none of us could remember Hitler. But occasionally, we'd slip back into the present to discuss articles from "The Week in Review" section of *The New York Times.* "You've got to keep current with what's going on in the outside world *now!*" was Peterson's battle cry. Then, in ten minutes, it was June 6, 1944, again, and we'd all be back on Omaha Beach while he replayed D-Day on the blackboard with sweeping gestures and sharp jabs of the chalk. It was entertaining in a way, but it didn't exactly bring us a step closer to the Outside World.

Strangely enough, it was Ellen who did that for me. One evening, during finals week last June, I was sitting at the kitchen table, running through my Spanish verb flash cards. Whenever my mind wandered, I could watch Liz out in the back yard. She seemed to be playing a lonesome version of "Mother, May I?" with herself.

38

The front door banged, and it was Ellen, hours early for her. "Mom's not home yet, is she?" Since it was just after eight, that was a pretty harebrained question. But then, Ellen was always hazy about the daily routine of our household. She pulled up a chair, and I got a good view of her. Her eyes were red and puffy.

"They've got him," she said, in a heavy whisper.

Well, I caught the general drift right then. After many weeks of noncommunication, we were going to be sisters-together again. The "him" was obviously Kevin Coleman, and Ellen needed a listening ear.

I felt the sudden impulse to turn bratty. So I swept the Spanish verb flash cards up from the table, palmed them into a pack, and shuffled them with a few extra flourishes, Mississippi Riverboat style. Ellen waited impatiently for me to settle down and listen nicely. Instead, I started dealing out two hands of flash cards.

"Care for a little five-card stud, lady?" I asked in my best underworld accent.

This performance had an unexpected effect on Ellen. Instead of yelling at me, she gave me this bewildered look. Then her face sagged in complete exhaustion. She looked exactly like a junior edition of Mom on a bad night, and almost as old. That settled me down. I dropped the remaining cards and edged back on the chair. "Sorry," I said in a small voice. "Who's got him?"

"The officials at the border. Kevin was making a routine crossing, and they stopped him on this side. They're holding him in some stinking jail until his case comes up. He's a political prisoner, that's what he is!" Ellen ran all this together in one long, gasping sentence. "What's he going to do, Maewest? He won't even have the money for a real lawyer. They assigned him one, but that's probably worse than nobody. They'll lock him up and let him rot. I know it." Then her face crumpled up. She put her head down on the table and began to sob.

Getting any more information out of her wasn't an easy job, but I was willing to try in order to stop the tears. They worried me. I couldn't remember ever seeing Ellen cry, even when we were kids. As it turned out, she didn't know much more. What information she had was sifted through the porous brain of Mitsy Decker. Mitsy had never been a particular friend of Ellen's until lately. But now she was, mainly because Mitsy had introduced her to Kevin. And it was Mitsy who'd arranged for Kevin to live out at her father's fishing shack—without her parents' knowing it. And Kevin had called her, asking her to break the news to Ellen and to send him his things.

There wasn't much to go on, but I tried to keep Ellen talking because she was about to edge over into hysteria. "Do his folks know? Maybe they can help."

"No, no," she said in a strangling voice. "They're dead. The Deckers' place was his only address. He doesn't have anybody but . . . me."

And Mitsy Decker, I thought, but I kept it to myself. This wasn't getting us anywhere, so I tried again. "Look, Ellen, this organization he works for. If they help conscientious objectors and army defectors and people like that, they'll have lawyers and money for bail. That's the way it works. They'll take care of him. After all, he's doing their work, isn't he? They have a responsibility for him."

This gradually began to calm her down, but I could tell she was feeling helpless and useless. The nearest border's a long way off.

The phone rang then, which is a fairly rare occurrence at our house. Ellen jumped up so fast her chair went over backwards. She looked at me for a second with a crazed kind of excitement in her eyes. "It's him," she said.

"No, it isn't, Ellen," I said, but she was out of the room and racing for the phone. I sat there hearing enough of Ellen's side of the conversation to know it was Mitsy and that she was heading our way.

When Ellen came back in the room, she was disappointed but not destroyed. Mitsy was coming by, and the two of them were going out to the cabin to pack up Kevin's things. They were going to send him his books and personal stuff and generally shape up the place so that Mitsy's father wouldn't notice he'd had a lodger out there. Mitsy had been anxious to get Kevin out anyway, now that summer was coming on.

I was getting pretty tired of being picked up and dropped. Besides, Mitsy Decker isn't exactly the most sympathetic character in the world to be stuck with when the chips are down. So I hinted that I might go along if she'd let me. Wonder of wonders, Ellen almost looked grateful. "Sure, Maewest, I could use a little moral support—even from you." It was about as sentimental a speech as I'd ever had from her lips. This could have developed into quite a touching scene, but then she said, "Say listen, how did you know it wouldn't be Kevin when the phone rang?"

"Well," I said, "he'd only be allowed one phone call, and he'd already made it."

She just looked at me for a minute and then burst out, "Dammit, Maewest, you're so . . . logical!" Then she started crying again and kept it up the whole time until Mitsy got there.

You know me, always so conscientious about looking after Liz. Well, I nearly shot off without a thought about her. At the last minute, while Mitsy was leaning on the horn out front, I scurried around to the neighbor lady who lives in the other half of our house and ask her to keep an eye on Liz for an hour or so. We planned to be back in plenty of time before Mom got home.

And in ten mintues the three of us were roaring along a country road west of town, heading for the lake. I was sandwiched into the front seat of the Decker Dodge between Mitsy and Ellen. Being out of the house with Ellen was novel enough, but to add to the effect, this was certainly the closest I'd ever been to Mitsy.

How shall I describe her? An odd case. Her parents aren't too bad off (Decker Feeds and Grain), but she's not within spitting distance of the Smart Set. It's either because she acts too tough or that she's too dumb, which in her case is no act. Probably a combination of both. Her two favorite expressions are:

1. "For cripe's sake."
2. "Listen, I've been around."

She used both a number of times on the way out to the lake. And to tell you the truth, that's about all I heard.

It was one of those early June nights when the light lingers on for hours. We missed the sunset which must have been spectacular, but there was still a pale glow in the west and a star or two just above the black silhouette of the trees around the lake. Then we entered the woods, and it was night in there.

The land around the lake is a private preserve, supposedly off limits to everybody except the people who own the cabins. It's sort of a club, but nothing fancy. A place where businessmen from town go out to fish and drink beer on the weekends. And where high school kids sneak in late at night. I'd heard stories about what goes on out there then, especially after prom night.

An old, rickety gate across the road loomed up at us. Mitsy pulled up, and Ellen jumped out to open it. Obviously, she'd done that before. From there on the road got steep, and our headlights picked up a gleam from the black water. It was a litle eerie, but interesting. We drove past Cottage numbers one through four, and then, Mitsy swerved off the road and drove up into the yard of number five.

When she killed the motor and the lights, we just sat there for a moment. It was so quiet you could hear the fish jumping in the lake. The trees shut out the last of the evening light, but there were little pinpoint flickers from the fireflies off in the woods. It was kind of a magic place—like nothing could ever get to you there. But then Mitsy said, "Come on, let's get this over with," and we stumbled Indian file toward the cabin.

Inside, the place was pitch-black. Worldly Mitsy and I lingered at the door, and she said, "I hope somebody remembered to bring matches." But Ellen was past us and swallowed up in the gloom.

"Just wait a minute," we heard her say. A match finally flared in the middle of the room, and the glow from a kerosene lamp dazed us. Ellen had known just where it was. She turned up the wick, and the flame bathed her face in a warm, yellow light. She wasn't pretty then, I thought. She was beautiful. And her face was streaked with tears.

The cabin was really just one room. There were two little push-out windows overlooking the lake with an old iron bedstead under them. In an alcove, there was a sort of thrown-together kitchen. It had a bottled-gas cookstove, and an old zinc sink with a pump, and a long drainboard for cleaning fish. A few battered pieces of porch furniture around the main part of the room and some old calendars on the walls. And that was it.

It definitely didn't have that lived-in feel. Kevin must be the tidy type—or cautious. Mitsy Decker's dad could have walked right in without knowing somebody was staying there. Lived in or not, I liked it in a way. It was more of a hideout than anything else, but I could imagine settling in down here. It was a little weird at night, but I thought I'd like it fine during the day. Just going around barefoot and listening to the wind in the leaves. Like Rima in *Green Mansions* or something like that. It would be great to bring Liz down here and let her paddle around in the lake. Trees, water, little snatches of blue sky—and no trouble.

But we had work to do. Mitsy was clearly going to be no help. She just stood around, managing to look both bored and cranky. Ellen reached under the bed without even looking and pulled out an old suitcase with straps. "All right, Maewest, go through the drawers in that dresser over there and make sure you get everything out." It was a different Ellen in that place. Sad and worried, but sort of in command, as if she was in the only home she could call her own.

"Yeah," Mitsy added unnecessarily, "don't leave anything around."

The top drawer was completely empty, which I thought might be clever Kevin's way of fooling anybody just having a casual snoop around. But the next drawer was full of sweat socks and underwear, all in neat little piles. This spooked me a little. Up till then, it had been a game, more or less, but here was actual evidence of Kevin in my hands. It was a little like opening a grave. Or, maybe, it made him seem more alive.

I stacked everything on top of the dresser and kept feeling around to make sure I hadn't missed anything. The light was pretty bad. Stuck in the corner of the drawer was something metal. It felt like a giant safety pin. I pulled it out. A wire something-or-other.

The next drawer had piles of sweaters—very conservative Ivy League goods. I scooped them all up. When I did, a whole blizzard of little, flimsy, white paper squares came flying out and scattered all over one end of the room. They settled on the floor like moths. Ellen was too busy trying to get everything into one suitcase to notice, but Mitsy, who was standing around doing nothing, was on to it in a minute.

"For cripe's sake," she said, "cigarette papers. Kevin's probably got pot around here, too. That's all I'd of needed is for him to get busted by the fuzz while he was out here."

Ellen whirled around at that and saw the papers. "Kevin doesn't smoke pot! He never has. I'd have known, wouldn't I?"

"Yeah," Mitsy said, "you'd of probably known all right."

It was a bad moment just when we didn't need one. I felt sort of guilty. For a second, I thought maybe Ellen would blame me. Maybe she'd think I was trying to stage an encore for my five-card-stud act. Anyway, I didn't see how a bunch of cigarette papers was any solid proof that Kevin had turned the place into an opium den or something. Leave it to lowlife Mitsy to see everything in the worst light.

But Ellen was just standing there holding a bunch of Kevin's paperback books, giving Mitsy the look that kills. Well, you could tell right off, Mitsy wouldn't put up with being at a disadvantage. She began to mutter something about how she'd smoked a little pot in her time and she was as broadminded as anybody, but . . . Then, she stalked over and just pushed me out of the way. "I'll clean this out myself. The kid might overlook something."

The kid! For two cents, I'd have yanked out a handful of her frizzy hair.

Then she saw the thing that looked like a giant safety pin, which I'd so conveniently put on top of the pile of sweat socks. She grabbed it up like it was the Hope diamond.

"Well, well, well. What have we here?" Frankly, I didn't know what we had here, and since it was giving her so much satisfaction, I wished I'd dropped it down behind the dresser when I had the chance. The tone of her voice brought Ellen straight over. Mitsy stuck the bent-wire thing right under her nose.

"So Kevin doesn't smoke pot, huh?"

Ellen looked as if she was just about at the end of her sanity. In a voice that would have warned off anybody but Mitsy Decker, she said, "No. Kevin doesn't smoke pot or drop acid or get high or anything you care to mention. He has told me he does not, and he *does not*."

"Then what's he doing with a roach holder?"

Mitsy had us both there, and well she knew it. Neither Ellen nor I knew what she was talking about, but Mitsy was glad to educate us. It's this wire contraption you hold a marijuana cigarette in so you can smoke it right down to the end without burning your fingers. And Mitsy was waving it around while she delivered her lesson like it was Exhibit A.

Well, if she was trying to add the final touch of misery, it worked. Ellen just went back to the suitcase and carried on with her packing like a robot woman.

"For cripe's sake, get those papers up off the floor," Mitsy barked, but I was already down on my hands and knees picking them up. When I had them all, I stood up. Mitsy was still fiddling with the roach holder. I just whipped it out of her hand and walked out of the cabin.

It was really night by then. I stood on the

47

front step until my eyes adjusted to the dark. Down by the lake, an old bullfrog was tuning up for a love song. I was in no hurry to go back inside. I walked across the little clearing and into the woods. A way in, I reached down for a rock I'd stubbed my toe on. There were probably snakes around and who knows what slimy things, but I didn't even think. I jammed the papers and the wire contraption down in the soft ,wet earth and put the rock back over them.

Then I went back and waited in the car.

From there, I could just see Mitsy and Ellen through the open door. They were bending over the table in the smoky light of the kerosene lamp. Mitsy was reading off Kevin's jail address from a little notebook, and Ellen was copying it with a felt-tipped pen on the side of the suitcase. From this distance, they almost looked friendly. Ha.

Deciding I'd already been as close to Mitsy as I cared to be, I climbed over into the back seat. And when they came out (not speaking to each other), Ellen swung the suitcase back by me. It was pretty quiet all the way to town. In fact, it was completely quiet. When we were nearly home, we stopped at a traffic light, and I could read the address on the suit case. I looked again. Kevin was being held in El Paso, Texas. That didn't seem to make any sense to me.

Claypitts is a lot closer to the Canadian border, like hundreds of miles closer. And everything I'd ever read about draft evaders and conscientious objectors said they went to Canada. There's an organization of people up there who help them. It's all organized. I'd never heard about anybody going over to Mexico by way of El Paso. Still, you never know. There was quite a bit we hadn't covered in Contemporary World Problems. I decided not to say anything to Ellen about it.

(A) she'd had enough for one night.

(B) she knows even less about the Outside World than I do.

We pulled up in front of our house. After we got out, Ellen leaned back and said, "You'll send this Railway Express tomorrow, won't you?"

"Yeah, yeah, sure," Mitsy grumbled.

"Better keep it hidden out in the garage or in the trunk so your parents won't see it."

"ALL RIGHT!" Mitsy snarled and gunned away from the curb.

On our way up to the front porch, Ellen put her arm around my shoulders. Another Famous First.

5 | Those first couple of weeks of the summer vacation were about as cheerful as the infamous Chinese Water Torture. Ellen spent most of the time lying across her bed, saying nothing and looking sick. Mom saw more of her than she had in years and took the opportunity to nag her about getting a summer job. I kept clear of both of them as much as humanly possible.

Until the day the letter for Ellen came. As it happened, I intercepted it at the mail box. When I saw the Texas postmark, I smuggled it up to her.

Now, since you're about to read the letter yourself, let's get one thing straight. I didn't make a detour into the kitchen and steam it open or anything like that. Ellen let me read it. Not then, but later. I guess it was the first and last letter she ever got from Kevin Coleman.

Dear El,

Time's about to run out on me. They're going to move me from this lockup to a federal pen someplace. They really threw the book at me this time, kid, and I guess there isn't anybody in the world who cares except maybe you. They'll probably read this letter and probably censor it. But it's worth a try even though everything I have to tell you is going to make

50

you hate me. Well, I guess it doesn't make much of a difference now to either one of us.

Remember how I used to call you Miss Innocent and how that made you raving mad? But you were. You believed everything I ever told you. It's just my luck the judge didn't.

I hate to tear down the big image you fell for. Now I wish I could have lived up to it. It wasn't just for your benefit so don't take it too much to heart. I was working your territory, but not for the draft dodgers. I was selling pot and whatever I could get my hands on to the kids at State U. I think every other scholar at that cow college is a head, so business was great. But the campus was hot so I came down your way. I was looking for a nice, safe place to work out of so Mitsy Decker's cabin looked like a perfect setup.

I needed all the cover I could get—hideout in the woods, short hair, button-down shirt, noble cause—the whole bit. I wish you wouldn't think it was just to psyche you out. It was business. I'd had a little trouble before, back east it was. One fine, one suspended sentence, a thirteen-month stretch for possession. I couldn't afford another bust. I guess this letter proves that.

Well, to make a long story short, they caught me at Customs coming back into El Paso from Juarez. I was way off my turf down here, but some of the raids up around Chicago had dried up my usual sources.

Remember how I used to tell you I was a *doer*, not a *talker*? Well, that much was true anyway. I drove all the way down here to try to line up some new contacts on the Mexican side. I found them all right with no sweat, though I think they were the ones who tipped off the Customs for a kickback. Anyway, I'd brought back some grass—it looked like the best I'd ever handled. Not much. They caught me with three kilos behind the dashboard—and believe me, they knew where to look. It wasn't much—not even seven pounds.

But, like I say, they threw the book at me when they had a look at my previous record. I was hoping for a trial in a Texas court for possession, but they wouldn't let it go at that. So it was the federal court and a drug-smuggling charge. They wouldn't even reduce it to importing marijuana without a license—not when they started checking my record.

So, El, it's ten years. And knowing me, not much time off for good behavior. But then, I guess you never did know me. And I guess it's just as well. It was great while it lasted, and where I'm going I'll have plenty of time to remember you. But you better forget me.

I'll always think of you as Miss Innocent.

So long,
Kevin

The weird thing about summer vacationtime is how good it looks till it get there. You know how it is. Everybody starts counting the days from Easter on. You sweat through finals (I got three A's and two B's that year, by the way). Then the glorious day finally comes when you clean out all the crud that's been moldering in the bottom of your locker since winter.

People who haven't said a civil word to you all year are running around banging you on the back and saying they'll see you again in the fall. And having you write in their yearbooks. Well, to tell you the truth, the only person who asked me to inscribe a book was Verna-Marie Scheibley. She rides the Consolidated District bus in from the country, and her feed-sack frocks keep me from being the worst-dressed member of the class. I tried to do the decent thing by Verna-Marie, but I haven't had much practice in writing in yearbooks. So all I could think of to say was:

Well, we made it through algebra.
Good luck in the future.

Sincerely,
Carol Patterson

Later, I heard she'd flunked algebra. See how it is? My heart's in the right place, but socially, I'm hexed.

Then the summer days seem to run together and stand still, all at the same time. If it hadn't been for Liz, I think I'd have tried sleeping straight through till Labor Day.

Kevin's letter really knocked Ellen out. But I expected her to snap back after a while. There was no earthly reason for her to be friendly with Mitsy Decker, of course. But I thought that sooner or later she'd be back in her BORN LOSERS, INCORPORATED windbreaker and down at McDonald's whooping it up with the rest of the gang. Weaker and wiser maybe, but still in there swinging. You know how it is: once a member, always a member. But it didn't happen.

You couldn't get her out of the house. And you couldn't get even an uncivil word out of her. It was like sharing your cage with a zombie. And to tell you the truth, I was hurt. I figured I was better than nothing when it came to having a friendly listening ear. But Ellen wasn't communicating at all.

Then one morning when I was trying my best to stay unconscious till noon, Liz woke me up. She had me half dragged out of bed before I could get my eyes open. And when I did, I saw she was scared. "Wake up, Carol," she said in this little whimpering voice. "They're going to hurt each other."

It was a battle, all right. I could hear Mom screaming and the sound of slaps. And Ellen screaming back and wailing. I wanted to pull the sheet over my head. But Liz's eyes were spilling over with tears.

I told her to stay upstairs, but of course, she didn't. She wouldn't let go of my hand. So the two of us got as far as the kitchen door, which was shut. But that was close enough.

One of the chairs scraped back, and I thought it was probably Mom sitting down. Maybe the worst of it was over. I wanted to pull Liz away and run out to the park or anyplace. But I don't think either one of us would have moved just then. It was quieter in the kitchen, but I could just barely hear Mom say, "What is it all for? I work myself half to death, and what is it all for?" It was a long moan, not really angry anymore. Worse than that—it was hopeless. And Ellen was sobbing. It was scarier than a fight, for some reason. I looked down at Liz and jerked my head to try and make her run on out the front way. But she just shook her head right back at me. She looked like a little owl, serious and smart.

Pretty soon, she pulled me back under the

stairway and made me bend over so she could whisper.

"I know what's the matter." She stared up at me to make sure I was paying attention. "Ellen's going to have a little baby." Then she really did look exactly like an owl with her eyes wide and wondering—but wise. Liz doesn't miss much, even when she's scared. I believed her. She wouldn't make up anything like that. So, I just nodded, and we started walking very quietly toward the front door. By then, we were both ready to clear out for awhile.

We never made it though. I guess it's just as well. I don't know what I'd have done wandering around the streets of Claypitts in broad daylight in my old, ripped, shorty nightgown. The kitchen door opened, and Mom was standing there. She must have heard us. "All right, you two better come back in here."

Even though Liz knew more than I did, I still wanted her out of it. But we walked back into the kitchen together. There was Ellen with her head down on the table, turned away from us. And all I could think was what a beautiful day this is. Why did it have to happen on such a beautiful day? The sun made Ellen's hair all lively with reddish lights.

"Well, if you haven't heard already, you'll have to know now," Mom said, as if Ellen wasn't even there in the room with us.

"We know," I said.

"Yes, and probably all the neighbors too, not that it matters. Sit down." You'd have thought she was mad at Liz and me, but, of course, every word she spoke was for Ellen's ears.

Liz perched up on a chair. She was very sober,

but you could tell she wasn't going to miss anything. The minute I sat down, it dawned on me this was the first time I could ever remember when we were all in the same room together. It took something like this.

But Mom was saying, "Ellen, sit up! I don't want you to miss any of this." Ellen did as she was told. Her face was sickly white and empty. "Look at your sisters. I want you to look at them and see what you've done to them!" This was going to be even worse than I thought. "I've tried to keep us together and make things right, and be in two places at once, and be two parents to you all, but nothing went right. I never did want any of you to have to grow up too quick, and I never wanted any of you to have to go through what I've had to go through. I wanted everything better for you three, and now—" That was as far as she got with that. Her voice cracked, and she just stopped dead and stared out the window like she might find an answer to all of this out there in the sunlight.

I guess Mom wanted to keep herself from crying again. I guess she thought giving Ellen the third degree would give her strength. So, she said, "Now, Ellen, I'm going to ask you once and once only, who is the boy?" I think my heart stopped then.

Ellen looked right at her and said, "It doesn't matter who he is. He's gone." Her eyes were dry, but I wanted to cry for her. I knew where he'd gone.

"I said I was going to ask you once," Mom said, and she was looking dangerous. "Now tell me."

There was a long silence then. But it was Liz

56

who broke it finally. Liz, in a little, firm voice: "It's Kevin. He lived in the woods."

Ellen turned slowly around toward Liz. I think that was the first time she every really, truly looked at her.

6 | We got through the rest of that summer. That's about all I can say for it. Broiling hot all the time, and nobody talked. At night, a mosquito or two would slip in through the torn screen wire on the bedroom window and buzz around. Believe it or not, I was glad to hear that sound. In a way, it was company.

Once, in August, we really did have company of a sort. Ellen went away just before school started. While the rest of her gang was gearing up for their senior year, Ellen was packing an old cardboard suitcase. But before she left, a lady came down all the way from Chicago.

She was from this home for unwed pregnant girls. It was one hundred and two degrees that day. Mom set up a big fan on the living-room floor that pulled in all the hot, dusty air from the street. She sat there on the edge of a chair in her regulation black dress with her mouth pulled into a tight line. Ellen stared into the fan, but she'd made the arrangements on her own, so she had to carry through. I was on the sofa with Liz mainly because neither one of us could think of anywhere else to be.

The lady from Chicago was sort of cool-looking and fresh. Miss Hartman was her name. She had on a yellow linen dress, and her hair was pulled back off her neck in a pretty twist. I don't know what I'd been expecting. Some big, gray-haired Amazon carrying a ring of keys on a leather strap around her waist or something. You know, like in *Jane Eyre*. But she was nice and normal. Once in a while, she'd smile over at Liz and me as she interviewed Ellen and tried to chat with Mom. I suppose the word for Miss Hartman was *discreet*.

But one thing she said that practically turned Mom to stone was, "Since there are so many fine families anxious to adopt children these days, I'm particularly glad that Ellen has not considered terminating her pregnancy."

I shot a look at Liz to see if she knew what that was all about, but I couldn't be sure. With Liz, you never know. So the moment passed, and the whole business could have been a lot worse, believe me. I guess, for Miss Hartman, it was all in a day's work.

I still couldn't quite believe that Ellen was going away. It wasn't as if I couldn't get along without her or anything. But then, we'd had our moment or two together. And besides, why on earth *should* she go? To spare the family name? Who cared about us anyway?

Maybe it was even then I had this nagging idea that Ellen *wanted* to go—not just because she'd be embarrassed around her so-called friends, but because she wanted to get away from us—from me and Mom and Liz.

After all, she'd shown quite a lot of unusual initiative. She'd gotten in touch with this un-wed mothers' place through the Salvation Army Family Service. Probably her doctor recommended it or something, but the point is, she planned it for herself. It was like a getaway.

The lady didn't stay too long. She had a paper for Mom to sign and printed instructions on how to find the place outside Chicago to give to Ellen. Then she turned again to Mom, who hadn't had much to say. "We'll take very good care of your daughter, you know. We have every facility and service. I'm sure you'll find that this is the right thing for Ellen, Mrs. Patterson."

And Mom only said, "Yes, I want her to go."

Ellen left on the evening bus to Chicago the day before school began. It makes a dinner stop at The Pull-Off Plaza, and passengers can get on there. I went with her to say good-bye. I thought maybe we'd ride out early with Mom in her car pool as she went to work. But she left while we were still upstairs. When we came down to the kitchen, there was a twenty-dollar bill in an envelope on the table. Across the outside of the flap, Mom had written, "Ellen, this is all I can spare right now." She hadn't even signed her name.

"I don't want it," Ellen said. "Leave it there."

I didn't tell her she'd need it. She knew that. I pretended I wasn't looking when she picked it up and put it in her purse.

We started out on foot, carrying the suitcase between us. Our fingers sort of nudged each other on the handle. Liz followed behind us for a couple of blocks. Finally, she turned back toward home. She was beginning to resent anybody having to look after her.

It's a long way out there. But who walks nowadays? The sidewalks peter out, and you have your choice of either trudging along at an angle on the cindery shoulder or up on the pavement where you can be knocked into the next world by some friendly passing motorist. We were nearly sideswiped by a nasty little Volkswagen with a PRAY FOR PEACE decal in the back window.

I tried concentrating on the scenery, which is a bad idea. Once you get past the houses and yards, there aren't any more trees. Just ragweed and hubcaps and that CLAYPITTS: PEARL OF THE PRAIRIE sign, along with others like CLAYPITTS WELCOMES INDUSTRY and CLAYPITTS: HAPPY HOME OF 13,000 FRIENDLY NEIGHBORS AND A COUPLE OF OLD SOREHEADS. And those spiky, little metal squares that tell you what day of the week the Kiwanis Club and the Rotarians meet, in case you're interested. You never really think how dumb and ugly signs are when you're whizzing by them in a car. For the full effect, try walking.

People even dump their garbage right out by the side of the road. They probably don't even stop their cars. Just slow down and let it fly. It's disgusting.

That cardboard suitcase was getting heavy by the time we made it to the parking lot. The bus was already there, but everybody was in The Pull-Off Plaza having supper. So, we just stood around. I knew Ellen was tense, but what could I say to make it better?

"It'll be late by the time you get up to Chicago. Think you can find your way all right?"

"Yes, I'll find it. Stop fussing."

The only other thing in the whole world I could think of to say was, "Go in and say goodbye to Mom," but I knew better than to try that.

Finally, the passengers started straggling back

toward the bus. Ellen took hold of my hand. She didn't look at me, but she held on tight. The bus driver was the jolly type with a skinny, little black uniform tie and a white shirt stretched over a big beer belly. He had a jovial word or two for every returning passenger. And when they were all on, he yelled up into the bus, "Next rest stop's at Watseka, so hold it till then." Ellen started to get on and turned back one last time. I had a sudden urge to kiss her good-bye or something, but she was a step above me. So I just said, "Write when you get settled. They'll let you write, won't they?"

"Of course, they'll let me write if I want to. It's not a jail." Then she looked over my head across the parking lot, and I turned around to see Mom outside the door of The Pull-Off Plaza. She was just standing there. Ellen looked at her a minute, with all that empty, black asphalt stretched out between them. Then she went on up into the bus, and the big door closed on her.

I watched the bus go lumbering off down the access road until it merged with the Interstate traffic and was only a row of red lights moving along higher than the rest of the cars. I stood there out at the edge of the parking lot, and I only turned back when I couldn't see the lights anymore. Mom was still standing by the restaurant door.

Now I know what I should have done, then. I should have gone over to her, even though there wouldn't have been anything to say. I could have gone in and sat at the counter for awhile and let her tell the waitress to fix me a soda or something. Just so she'd know I was there and that we were still a family or something like that. But I didn't. I just walked off the way Ellen and I had come. Maybe Mom didn't care. Maybe she wasn't even thinking about me.

I walked back on the opposite shoulder of the road because I knew there'd be places on the other side where you could see our footprints, going out. I took my time, looking at all those repulsive signs again and getting cinders in my shoes.

It's funny what you think about at times like that. I was in no hurry to get home, and yet, I wouldn't have been too surprised to find out our half of the house had just crumbled quietly away. With just a pile of plaster and old bricks heaped up where the basement should be. It was crazy, maybe, but I was beginning to think that we were all starting to drift away from the little we had together to the nothing we'd have without each other. It wasn't much that held us together—just spit and string, mostly, but it was something. Or, at least, it had been.

By now, Ellen was already miles up the road, going off alone to have a baby she'd have to give away to strangers. And Mom was back at her post, saying things like, "I'll have a table for you in just a minute," to people who never even gave her a second look. And Liz, all by herself, carrying on long conversations with imaginary playmates. But mostly, I thought about Ellen. That song the Beatles used to sing kept going around and around in my head, the one that says,

She's leaving home after living alone
For so many years, Bye, Bye

63

Not that I wasn't feeling pretty sorry for myself, too. I'd have been grateful for the sound of just one human voice, no matter what it said.

And then I heard it. And it said: "Hey, girl, get out of my zinnias!"

Sure enough, I'd tracked halfway through a zinnia bed. It was just a little square of flowers in front of a filling station, wedged in between the driveway and the road. It stopped me dead. I'd managed to mess up the only beauty spot in that entire polluted neighborhood. Who expects flowers, for Pete's sake, in the middle of that part of town?

And in front of an OKLAHOMA PETROLEUM: THE MOTORIST'S BEST FRIEND station, at that. I was afraid to move, even though I saw the attendant was heading my way. If he had blood in his eye, I knew it'd be my type.

He wasn't much older than I was, as it turned out, and not much taller. He was wearing a pair of bib overalls in the OKLAHOMA PETROLEUM colors and no shirt. He was on the skinny side, but his arms looked pretty sinewy. And like every filling station attendant that ever was, he had very neat hair (his was whitish-blond and on the long side, but *extremely* neat) and very dirty hands. I was expecting the worst, like he might pick me up and toss me out into the middle of the highway. So I just stood there, rooted to the spot, you might say.

But when he got up close, he said, "Hey, girl, you sick or something? Come on up to the station, and I'll give you a glass of water or a Coke." I didn't move, not wanting to plow up the rest of the flowers. "Come on, jump."

He held out an arm and hoisted me over onto the pavement with ease.

The inside of the station was very clean, with pyramids of blue-and-white oilcans neatly arranged along the walls. Everything had a bright bluish cast from the fluorescent lighting. He'd been drinking coffee out of a giant mug that said "Jerry" on it when I'd sent him hustling out to the flower bed.

I told him my name so he wouldn't keep calling me "girl." And he told me he was Jerry Rodebaugh. I knew the name. The Rodebaughs are a big tribe of country people. You see their name on mailboxes all over the county. The thing about it was I liked him right from the start, even considering I was desperate for a little company. He was nice about the zinnias and said they were hardy, and if exhaust fumes wouldn't kill them, then neither would I.

The thing I noticed about him right away was his pride. Not snotty, stuck-up pride. Real pride. He was proud of those zinnias, which he'd planted himself. And he talked about some melon plants he'd set out behind the station which weren't doing too well because they like sandy soil, but it was clay back there. He was proud of the whole filling station, even though he was only the night attendant. He showed me the holdup-proof safe which he was so pleased with you'd think he had the patent on it. It was just like a little metal plate set in the floor under the desk with a slot in it to take the folding money. And a sign bolted low down on the wall that said THIS IS A SEALED SAFE. ATTENDANT HAS NO KEY.

OKLAHOMA PETROLEUM didn't have too many

customers that evening. So we talked. To tell you the truth, this is about as long a conversation as I ever had with a boy. I told him about Mom and Liz and some, but not all, about Ellen. It wasn't that I was ashamed of her or anything. But Mom always says, "Don't air your dirty laundry in public." Maybe I'm more like her than I care to admit.

At nine-thirty, Jerry went out to take a reading on the pumps and coil up the air hose. He took a quick look at his bruised zinnias, too, I happened to notice. Since it was closing time, I started to leave, but he said he'd drive me home.

He had an old Plymouth with a roll bar and a big slab of wood bolted on in place of a front bumper. "I bought her off a guy who drove her in the stock car races. Plenty of life in her yet. I take her out on service calls. She's better than the tow truck." Then, suddenly, we were quiet all the way home. It was a little strained, which was funny, considering we'd been blabbing away all evening. But driving home together was more like a date. Not that this was quite how I'd pictured my first date. In fact, I'm not sure I ever had pictured my first date.

When we got home, I jumped out so he wouldn't think he'd have to walk me up to the door. "Well," I said, "see you in school, maybe."

"Yeah," Jerry said, "I drop in occasionally." Then he gave me a big grin and tooted the horn a couple of times when he got down to the corner.

Upstairs, Liz was already in bed and asleep. Probably trying to prove she can be responsible for herself and go to bed at a decent hour. In a way, I wanted to wake her up and tell her about Jerry. But then, I thought, she's wise enough. If there'll ever be anything worth knowing, old Liz will find it out.

7 | I spent quite a lot of time that first week of September training my eyes to stop looking for Jerry Rodebaugh around every corner in the school. Just as well. He wasn't there. I even went to the trouble of looking at the Official Absentee List, just to make sure some cruel fate wasn't causing us to miss each other in passing. It wasn't. His name turned up regularly on the list of the missing: RODEBAUGH, J.—usually misspelled by the idiot in the Attendance Office.

Claypitts has only one high school, naturally. And since it's a three-year institution, we tenth-graders are the lowliest of the low. I can handle that but finding my way around a new building shakes me up a little. With my wardrobe, I'm not exactly anxious to make a dramatic late entrance into any class.

Don't think starting high school and spending one evening with the opposite sex afflicted me with amnesia. I slept next to Ellen's empty bed. (Why didn't I take her bed and sleep next to the window, I wonder?) I wore Ellen's old gym suit to P.E. I ran home from school to check the mail on the off chance that she'd written. I even missed being called Maewest, if you can believe that.

But there were other things to think about to make that fall different. New school, new classes, new teachers. And this nagging daydream that Jerry Rodebaugh might roll back into my life in his battered, beloved Plymouth and carry me off. You know: a new version of *Sleeping Beauty*. Like "Wideawake Ugly."

And something else too. Just when I was about to expire from loneliness, I got a friend. Friend in need is friend indeed about sums it up. We were never what you'd call best buddies, but she was a very good friend to me. Her name's Shirley Gage, and of all things, she's the preacher's daughter. I sat next to her in art class, which was my once-a-week elective.

I figured Art would be relaxation time—a little finger-painting therapy and a few soothing turns of the pottery wheel. Don't you believe it. The teacher was one Miss Mergenthaler and her philosophy was FREE EXPRESSION IF YOU EXPRESS WHAT I APPROVE OF. Also BE CREATIVE OR I'LL FLUNK YOU. Also CLEAN OUT THOSE BRUSHES OR I'LL JAM THEM DOWN YOUR THROAT. She never exactly said any of this, but you got the idea. She never exactly said anything. She roared. And she was built like a Mack truck. Strong football players quivered. The only person in the art room who didn't was Shirley Gage.

Luckily, I sat next to her. When Mergenthaler started raging, Shirley just watched her, looking mildly interested. You'd think Mergenthaler would notice and try to get her for it, but she never bothered Shirley. There was a sort of truce there I never quite figured out.

Shirley is cool—supercool—without trying. I guess being a preacher's kid has made her kind of a public character, at home anywhere. She knows everybody, and everybody knows her, so she's just In generally without being In with any particular group.

We had life drawing during the first art session. We all sat at slanting drawing boards in a hollow square. In the middle was a big table with legs heavier than Mergenthaler's. She told Herb Whitby to get up on the table the first day. He's a first-string halfback, and it was then I first noticed that Mergenthaler could make strong males cringe.

"Okay, Whitby, get up on the table!" Herb's built even more like a Mack truck than you-know-who (and he looks a lot better), but he's the retiring type. Sort of modest and extremely uncoordinated except on the football field. He looked at Mergenthaler like she was the coach and jumped up from his seat, but it didn't dawn on him until she'd thundered a few more commands that he was supposed to get up on the table and strike a pose for us. Talk about mortified. He wanted to die.

He slipped getting up on the table, which caused Mergenthaler to roll her eyes. It would have made for a good laugh all around except we were on his side. When he got up there, his head almost brushed the ceiling. He slouched and looked miserable.

"Okay, Whitby, so you're not a professional model. We can see that. But do something. Assume a football stance. Anything. Flex those famous muscles!"

Then she turned on us. "Pick up your charcoal and loosen up!" We had no idea what she was talking about. She had a piece of charcoal in her hand, and started swinging her arms in big, athletic circles. "Loosen up," she boomed,

"Loooooosen up!" This caused a very few stifled chuckles at the far end of the room.

"Swing those arms! EVERYBODY! With charcoal, you work loose. You're not sewing on a button, you're sketching the human body. To work loose you've got to *be* loose. So LOOOOSEN UP!" She made us start swinging our arms around. It was sort of embarrassing, but it took the heat off Herb Whitby, who was looking down on us all from the table, somewhat dazed.

She bullied him into going down on one knee and flexing his right arm until his T-shirt sleeve strained. Then she made him freeze. "Begin!" We fell to it. My charcoal kept crumbling off in big pieces. I got nowhere. Well, I got part of his arm, sort of, but I couldn't get it connected up with a body.

All the while, Mergenthaler stalked around the room behind us in her ground-grabber space shoes with arms locked behind her back. I was sweating away over Herb's biceps when a big hand shot over my shoulder and grabbed the paper off my board. Mergenthaler's voice blasted right into my ear, "START OVER! THAT'S HOPELESS!" which caused a general stirring of insecurity around the room.

That tended to send me into shock, but I could tell Mergenthaler had moved on and was behind Shirley Gage, so I hazarded a quick glimpse at Shirley's drawing board. Then I looked again. Shirley wasn't sketching Herb. She didn't even have a piece of charcoal in her hand. Instead, she had a canvas stretched over her drawing board with tacks. She was calmly priming it with white paint, very carefully stroking it with a small brush—dead-white primer on

71

the dead-white canvas. Mergenthaler hesitated behind her a moment and then moved on.

While I was absorbing this and Herb Whitby was probably developing a charley horse to end his gridiron career, Mergenthaler continued making the rounds of the busy sketchers. Directly across the room from Shirley and me, she stopped suddenly behind Rupert Renfrew.

Rupert's chief trait is that he's always been the smallest kid for his age in the entire Claypitts school system. His feet dangled down below the drawing board, clearing the floor by a good six inches. He looks like a scared puppy, and he's always been too little to pick on. Until now.

Small as he is, he began shrinking when he felt Mergenthaler's hot breath on his neck. The room was especially quiet just then. I think everybody's charcoal was suspended in mid-stroke.

"NOW HERE'S SOMETHING OF ARTISTIC MERIT!" You can't pretend to ignore a voice like that. She reached over Rupert's head, but instead of snatching his paper and crumpling it up, she very carefully lifted it off the board. "OH YES, INDEED!" Mergenthaler was obviously pleased, but it was a nasty kind of pleased. She plowed to the center of the room right up to Herb, and said, "So, Mr. Touchdown, look what YOU inspired!" Then she opened Rupert's sketch for Herb to see. His eyes bugged out, and he went bright red. Even his arms blushed. He looked at the paper for a moment, then he looked away, straight ahead.

Mergenthaler turned to the rest of us. Without a word, she held up the sketch and walked all the way around the room in front of us.

It was a good likeness, all right. Even the face looked like Herb. It was a beautiful sketch —strong and real. And it pictured Herb Whitby naked as a Greek statue.

This caused some sickening giggles as Mergenthaler made the rounds with it, but mostly there was silence. When she held it in front of Shirley Gage's nose, Shirley looked up briefly, murmured, "Very good," and went back to her canvas priming. This took the wind out of Mergenthaler's sails. Mercifully, the bell rang.

We started to troop out, all except Rupert, who stayed slumped in his chair, small and hopeless. The rest of us avoided looking in his direction, but Shirley walked over to him. I only heard her first words because I was anxious to get out of there: "Nice work, Rupe, I'll never get past the still-life stage myself. Never can seem to get the human body to come alive." My last glimpse was of Rupert looking up at Shirley, cautiously pleased, seeing if she really meant it. She did.

A couple of days after that bad scene, I was in the cafeteria having my brown-bag sandwich and a box of milk. I was holed up in my usual spot down at the end of an empty table with all the gangs and groups whooping it up merrily all over the rest of the room.

Now I'd never had more than a word with Shirley Gage. I didn't suppose she'd even noticed that we sat next to each other in Art. Suddenly there she was, plopping her tray down right

73

across from me when she could have joined any table in the cafeteria.

"How's it going, Carol?" You could have knocked me over with the proverbial feather. Before I knew it, we were carrying on like old buddies. She's a junior, so she knows the ropes, and we were having a general sort of conversation about the ins and outs of Claypitts High. She's the kind of person who can explain things to you without making you feel like an imbecile. And since Art was our only class together, I edged the conversation around to that first session. What I really wanted to know was her plan for the canvas she was working on so independently. She said she was going to do a painting in oils for her father to hang in his study.

"What's it going to be of?"

"Well, now," Shirley said, "that remains to be seen. It's going to take me the full year to finish it."

I found that a little bit unusual, to say the least, particularly since Mergenthaler clearly had quite a number of required projects mapped out for our class. "You see it's like this," Shirley said. "Mergenthaler tends to be on the difficult side, but if she sees someone really working steadily on a major project, I expect she'll keep her distance. So I intend to make mine last."

"The whole year?"

"The whole year."

While I was digesting this inventive bit of strategy, it occurred to me to make an uncharitable comment or two on Mergenthaler's teaching technique, especially what she did to Rupert Renfrew.

I expected Shirley to agree wholeheartedly that Mergenthaler was a sadistic fiend who ought to be drummed out of the faculty, if not out of town. As I should have known, though, Shirley had her own viewpoint. "She's just misplaced."

"How do you mean?"

"I mean she probably wanted to be a real artist and didn't make it. So now she has to teach art and she hates to teach. She's just the wrong person for the job, so she's always in a foul mood."

Now, this made a lot of sense. Even so, I'd have enjoyed condemning Mergenthaler to Eternal Damnation without giving a thought to what might have made her the wretch she is. Even trying to figure people out was pretty new to me. I was impressed that it wasnt particularly new to Shirley.

It crossed my mind to tell her the story of Kevin Coleman to hear what insights she might have into him. But we never got around to that. Instead—you guessed it—before that lunch hour was over, I was blurting out all about my Great Meeting with Jerry Rodebaugh. She seemed to know who he was. She knows everybody. And she didn't laugh at me or make any big deal of it. She just listened. Believe me, you don't meet a good listener every day of your life.

8 | I'm a pushover for other people's houses. The day Shirley asked me to come home with her after school, I was very flattered. I tried to act casual, but I guess it was the first time I'd been in anybody's house since way back in the fourth grade. That time, I went to Laurie Pence's luxurious layout.

The Gages live in the house on the back lot of the Methodist Church. The parsonage has a sort of institutional look about it, built out of the same brown brick as the church. "It comes with the job," Shirley said.

Anybody's house looks good to me compared to my own, but still the parsonage was definitely on the drab side. Trellis paper in the living room with brown roses on it and *The Last Supper* over the fireplace. Nothing quite matched, but it was sort of dignified and very solid. On the spinet piano, there were a couple of photographs in silver frames, one of Shirley and one of another girl, older, who looked something like her. "My sister," Shirley said.

Under the stairway was a little squirrel's nest of a room, the minister's study. He was out making hospital calls, so we looked inside. It was full of books, piled on the floor, on the desk, everywhere. On one wall there was an old, yellow engraving of the Methodist Church. "That's what I'm going to replace with my

76

painting," Shirley said. "Can't help but be an improvement, can it?"

The dining room was very stiff, with high, carved wood chairs around the table. But I like dining rooms, mainly because we have to eat in the kitchen. Off that room was a glassed-in sun porch, but blinds were pulled down over all the windows. It was so dim in there I almost didn't see Mrs. Gage, stretched out in a chair with her feet up on an ottoman. She was a very faded lady in a vague print dress with a lacy handkerchief sticking out of the neck. She had a wet washcloth folded over her forehead. When Shirley introduced us, she said she was glad to meet me and sorry that she was a little under the weather. Her voice had a way-off-in-the-distance sound about it.

Upstairs, Shirley's room looked like Shirley—crisp, comfortable, and no flounces. No white-canopied bed either, of course. When we settled down to a couple of cokes, I asked her if her mother was sick, and she said only on Ladies' Sewing Circle days.

"You mean she fakes it?"

"No, Mother would think that was dishonest. But she hates playing the preacher's-wife role, so she really *is* sick on Sewing Circle days. It just works out that way. She'll be on the road to recovery by dinner time."

And I guess she was. When I was ready to leave that afternoon, I could hear Mrs. Gage out in the kitchen rattling pots and pans and singing "Blessed assurance, Jesus is mine" in a very pretty soprano voice.

But before I left, Shirley and I had a talk that made me feel a lot less alone. Somehow or other, conversation came around to her sister. Actually, it started with college. I told her I wasn't planning on going, and she said there might be a way, even if I had to work a few years first, which was a thought. Then I happened to ask her if her sister was away at school.

"No," she said, "Margaret's married. She didn't go to college. She couldn't."

The only reason I could think of for a preacher's kid not going to college was that she was too dumb, which, you'll be glad to know, I was careful not to say. "Margaret had to get married the summer before she was supposed to enter."

The conversation didn't end there, but even if it had, I'd have been given plenty to think about. Now I've got enough sense to know that Ellen wasn't the only girl in the world who got pregnant without being married. As the saying goes, "It happens in the best of families." But you don't expect it to happen in the preacher's family. At least I didn't. And there was another thing too. I already looked up to Shirley—the way she was wise about people without showing off or acting like she knows it all. And what she told me about her sister sort of drew us together. I even asked her who the boy was before I realized it sounded exactly like Mom talking.

"She married a guy who still had a couple of years of college to finish. So Margaret went to college all right, but not to study. They live in a trailer off campus and things are pretty rough, but I think they'll make it. He works nights, but Margaret can't do much but stay home and look after the baby. Even if she had a job, they'd have to pay a sitter. It's not much fun for her, but she's managing. Besides, she has to keep up a front for Mother and Father when she comes home to visit. You can imagine the whole thing was quite a blow to them."

I couldn't really imagine how the preacher's family reacted to something like that, and I must have looked blank because Shirley went on. "Mother developed the longest headache in history, but I think Father took it harder. You know he spends his life hearing other people's problems. It was tough for him to handle one that close to home. But these things work out. As far as my parents are concerned, having a grandchild just about makes up for anything."

There was a slightly awkward little pause then, while I thought about Mom. Up till then, all I'd considered was how Ellen was going to have to give her baby up and go on as if nothing had ever happened. But for the first time, it dawned on me that Mom was going to have a grandchild she'd never get to see. No matter how mad she was at Ellen or just plain discouraged, maybe what hurt the most was that she'd never see her own grandchild. She might not even know if it was a boy or a girl.

It was that old familiar feeling again—that nobody has problems as hopeless as ours. Other people manage to get some satisfaction out of life, but maybe people like Ellen and Mom and Liz and me—maybe we're doomed.

"Sorry," Shirley said, "about the grandchild bit, I mean. That's the way it worked out with our family, but that's not the only way."

"You mean you know about *my* sister?"

"Well, it's a small town, isn't it? Not too likely

a place for keeping a secret. Besides, Ellen's only a year ahead of me. I've always known who she is. That high school may look big to you now, but after a while, it starts shrinking. And you have to be stone deaf not to hear gossip. You and Ellen aren't invisible you know. Carol."

She'd put her finger on it. That's just exactly how I'd always felt, about myself I mean. Invisible. Like nobody even knew I was there. I couldn't decide whether what Shirley said made me feel better or worse. Better, I guess, because she took the trouble to break through my shell —crack it a little, anyway. And she did it without hurting—much.

Not too long after that day, she did something else for me, too. At least, I think she engineered it. Coincidences happen, but I doubt that this was one of them.

To tell you the truth, I was still feeling fairly invisible, Shirley or no Shirley. My hopes of seeing Jerry faded a little more each day as his name continued turning up on the absence list. I sort of walked through the daily routine. Shirley was right. Claypitts High did begin to shrink. I was already tired of all the new faces before September was over.

Then finally a postcard came from Ellen. It was addressed to me. I guess I should have been thrilled. (How often do I get mail?) But I wished she'd addressed it to Mom, too. Here's all it said:

Dear Maewest,

I'm getting settled in. It's not too bad a place, but it's no finishing school either, ha ha. I'm feeling all right and the food's eatable. We're not supposed to mention our hometowns to each other here, but who wants to hear about Claypitts anyway. Personally, I don't care if I never see that dump again.

More later,
Luv,
Ellen

Glad as I was for even that much news from Ellen, it gnawed at me. I knew Mom read it, too. It was right out there in plain sight on the hall table one afternoon when I got home from school. But she and I still weren't able to talk about Ellen. Sometimes, I'd rehearse all kinds of ways of bringing her up, like, "Say, Mom, we ought to be hearing from Ellen again pretty soon. It's been a while since she's written." Oh, I devised all kinds of supercasual, off-the-cuff ways of introducing the subject. But of course, when it came time to say them, I couldn't. They didn't even sound right to me. And that line in the postcard about never caring to see Claypitts again. Whatever Ellen thought she meant by that, you couldn't shrug it off.

I was beginning to think that Ellen was mixed up in Mom's mind with my father. Like when people let her down, that's it. Finished. Don't talk about them; try not to think about them. They hurt you once, and once is enough without digging it up again. Words won't help.

Maybe that's the way Mom felt about it. And maybe words don't really help. But, believe me, neither does silence.

What was going to happen to Ellen after

she'd had her baby began preying on my mind. I swore a solemn oath to myself not to talk to Shirley about it. I didn't want her to start thinking I was using her as my own personal Guidance Counselor. And then, I decided to break my solemn oath and bring it up the next time we had lunch. I have this very strong character, have you noticed?

So when I caught a glimpse of Shirley way down at the end of the cafeteria at "our" table, I by-passed the milk line and made a beeline back there. I was practically on top of her before I saw she wasn't alone. Sitting across from her was—gasp—Jerry Rodebaugh. They were chatting away, cool as you please. Oh, did I handle that beautifully! For openers, I dropped my sandwich on the floor. Oh, I was Miss Sophisticated. You'd have been proud to know me.

Somewhere way off in the cosmic distance, Shirley's voice was saying, "Carol, I guess you know Jerry." I hope I answered. I hope I said yes. I guess I did. I'm not sure. I remember clearly what he said though: "Sure I had to fish her out of my zinnia patch."

Shirley acted as if this was a reasonable enough rendezvous. And in true-blue Shirley fashion, she carried it off as if she hadn't already heard that fascinating social note from me.

Since the conversation was in danger of running out of steam, Shirley started giving Jerry a little mild digging about his offhand attitude toward school attendance. She suspected (and I was positive) that he'd missed the entire first four weeks of school. He pleaded guilty

82

to this charge. "Since you're the ace mechanic of OKLAHOMA PETROLEUM, seem to me you'd at least come to school for the shop courses," Shirley observed. "There is such a thing as 'Auto Mechanics' you know."

"I've heard tell they give that here," Jerry replied innocently. "In fact, I believe I took it year before last."

"In fact," I heard myself saying, "you could probably teach it."

"You said it. I didn't," he answered, giving me this large, knee-quivering grin.

And then suave Shirley who must have planned this meeting as only she could (but who denied it when questioned later) just melted away. One minute she was there. The next minute, Jerry and I were alone at the table. She may have said something vaguely like, "There's Emily Ryan over there. I need to get the trig assignment from her." Or maybe she didn't even say that. She just vanished.

And after a short pause, while Jerry rearranged the salt and pepper shakers and I did my best to chew through a bone-dry sandwich without benefit of milk, he said, "I hear they're going to have the bonfire and Harvest Moon Dance again this year."

Silence.

"Care to go?"

I'll end this scene right now. I don't even want to remember how fast I said yes.

9 | When I told Mom I was going to the bonfire that night, I didn't mention anything about the Harvest Moon Dance. Which means, of course. I didn't mention that Jerry was going to take me. I didn't mention Jerry—*period*.

And eight o'clock took its time about getting there. I can tell you. I filled in the time the best way I knew how by trying on my best dress. It's sort of a bad plaid, and it was formerly known as "Ellen's best dress." It has an even longer history than that, but Ellen is as far back as I can trace it. All I can be sure of is that it's been around more than I have—and it's beginning to look it.

"How come you're not wearing Levis to the bonfire?" Liz wanted to know, who was stationed on her bed, watching every move I made.

"Because I'm wearing a dress," I explained.

"Can I come with you?" Now that really got to me. Remember how I used to hate it when Ellen never paid any attention to Liz? I was getting just as bad. Worse, because Liz expected a little notice from me. So I stopped trying to beautify myself and sat down on the bed next to her and told ALL.

Now any regular little kid would start carrying on and teasing me because I was having a real date for once in my life. You know, the usual, repulsive, little-sister bit. But Liz just absorbed it all with great interest. She was quite impressed. I promised that I'd tell her everything that happened when I got home, little knowing how much there'd be to tell. This seemed to satisfy her completely. And since she was going to be stuck at home with the usual nothing to do, I pointed out that, in a few years, she'd be going out on a date herself.

"You mean I can wear the dress then?" For an answer to that, I just grabbed her and gave her ten or twelve kisses and hugged the breath out of her. She probably thought I was deranged.

When the doorbell rang. I told Liz to skip down and let Jerry in. She shot down those stairs two at a time, and I just happened to hear her first words of greeting to him: "Carol's got on her best dress." I cringed.

But after I'd hung around the bedroom a minute and a half, developing cold feet, I went downstairs. Liz was practically in Jerry's lap, entertaining him with all the tidbits of grade-school life. I especially remember one line, "My teacher, Miss Grissom, has warts."

So, by the time I entered the scene, they were old buddies. "Have a good time," Liz said as we left. "I'll leave the porch light on." That kid is beginning to sound distinctly matronly.

The bonfire was great. There was something magical about it. The haze of wood smoke in the air, the flames reflecting on the row of yellow maples at the end of the schoolyard, and on the faces of the kids. It was a chilly night, but somehow cozy, like the bonfire was a single candle flame, but big enough to warm us all. It was the center of the pep rally for Saturday's game. Occasionally a member of the team, like Herb Whitby, got hoisted up and carried around the fire to receive a special ovation. There were organized cheers, and everybody sang the school song. For a little while, that mass of kids, the front row in the light, the rest in the dark, were all friends. We all belonged to each other. It only lasted minutes, but you could feel it.

There was a snake dance then, weaving in long loops around the yard as the fire burned down to a big, glowing mound. The line led over to the school where the dance was starting. The gym was beginning to throb with amplified rock.

"Want to go in for a while?" Jerry said. I realized we'd been standing there in the crowd holding hands. I hadn't even noticed.

I didn't much want to go inside and break the mood. Somehow, it would seem too much like school. The same old faces you see every day, but not all together in the way they'd been around the bonfire. "We could go for a ride instead," Jerry said. I figured he didn't want to dance. I couldn't really picture him on the gym floor milling around and banging into everybody else to a rock beat.

"Okay," I said, "but I can't stay out too late." I decided I had to keep a grip on myself and be sure to be home before Mom got there.

We drove out toward the lake. I remembered the last time I'd been over that road—going out to Kevin's hideout. Jerry's a good driver, of course, easy on the corners, with a keen eye for loose gravel. The headlights made a tunnel ahead of us. Once, a rabbit ran halfway out into the road, right into our path. The headlights dazed it so that it froze, one eye bright as a diamond. Jerry touched the brake and flicked the dimmers. The rabbit leaped away into the hedge in a single bound.

There was some old-fashioned 1940's music playing low on the radio. I'd cast a glance at Jerry's profile every once in a while. He's not really what you'd call star quality, but he has a good profile—and that hair that shows blond even in the dark.

There wasn't much conversation, not that we needed it. It was almost as if we got all our talking done that first night we met. Still, there were things I wanted to know about him. I'm not the world's champion at what's known as "drawing people out." Now, Shirley would have had him neatly psyched-out with an absolute minimum of effort to all concerned. But not yours truly. Nevertheless, I plunged right in.

"What do you want to do when you get out of school?" (Pretty bad, wasn't it? Especially considering he's a recognized truant—practically a dropout. But it was all I could think of.) It sounded suspiciously like, "What do you want to be when you grow up?"

"Something to do with cars, I guess," he said. "That's all I know." From there, the conversation veered away from the future and into the automotive world. And I got a lesson on such matters as three-carburetor manifolds, camshafts, RPM's, braking distances, high-compression heads, and linkage systems. It ended where it began with him saying, "I'm nothing but a grease monkey, past, present, and future."

There's something to be said for knowing what you are, I guess. Maybe, I wish I knew myself that well. But I couldn't help but feel there was more to Jerry than he thought. For some reason, I kept remembering that little bed of flowers he had encouraged in front of the filling station and the melon patch behind.

He braked and started to turn at the crossroads where the lane straight ahead leads down to the cottages around the lake. Suddenly, I had this thought. I remembered that night Ellen and Mitsy Decker and I went down to the cottage, and I wanted to see it again, with Jerry this time. I remembered liking the place.

"Let's drive on in," I said. It was an innocent suggestion, even though the lake's a well-known, late-night parking spot for dating couples. But I said it without thinking about that. Maybe it sounded like the wrong kind of invitation, but I didn't think Jerry would take it that way.

We drove in as far as the gate, which was standing open. I didn't think anything about it at the time. It seemed too early in the evening for anybody to be down there. It looked deserted enough. Most of the cabins were boarded up for the winter, and the ground was heaped with dead leaves. There really was a harvest moon, low and yellow, and it showed through the nearly bare branches. We pulled up in front of the Deckers' cottage.

I guess I realized then why I'd wanted to come here with Jerry. We sat there in the dark, and I told him about Ellen and Kevin Coleman. The whole thing from beginning to end. I didn't know if he already knew any of the story or not. I didn't care. I wanted to tell him myself.

Now I know it's not exactly the thing you talk about on a first real date—that your sister's in a place for unwed mothers-to-be and the boy who got her in trouble (as the saying goes) is in jail. But it seemed right telling him, especially telling him from my point of view.

Because in the last few weeks, especially after that postcard from Ellen, I was worried about what would happen next. Since I never got it talked out with Shirley, I needed to get it said to somebody.

Well, after I got that out of my system, we sat there awhile, listening to the quiet of the place. I didn't feel much better for telling it. It dawned on we that maybe Jerry only heard parts of the story and not others. But when he spoke finally, I knew it was all right. "You're Carol, not Ellen," he said. "I know that." And then, he kissed me.

It was a clear night, but as corny as it sounds, I'd have seen stars anyway. I wanted it to last, and it did. But finally, I pulled myself together and said, "I'd better be getting home." And Jerry said something very good to hear.

"All right. I better get you back on time so we can have more nights like this." By then, my thoughts had shifted from Ellen's future to my own without much hesitation.

As Jerry switched on the ignition, I happened to see something that practically made my hair stand on end. The car was headed directly at the Deckers' cabin door. That door began to open. It only opened a few inches; I don't even know what made me notice it. Jerry didn't. When he turned on the headlights, the cabin door banged shut. "Let's get out of here," I whispered. "Somebody's in that cabin." He didn't think so, but I did, and I wasn't for hanging around long enough to find out for sure. For one lunatic second, I imagined it might be Kevin Coleman, escaped from jail and back in his old haunt. Whoever or whatever it was, Jerry couldn't get that old Plymouth turned around fast enough to suit me. Talk about breaking a romantic mood!

As we swung around up the lane and back to the gate, the headlights caught a flash of chrome. There was a car pulled off the road in the trees. It was pretty well tucked away, and we must have passed it on the way in without noticing. Jerry saw it too, so he was more or less convinced I hadn't been having hallucinations about the cabin door.

Out of the trees and back on the county road, Jerry turned right, taking the long way back to town. It was only a little after ten, so there was no hurry. There isn't what you'd call a scenic route among all the roads around Claypitts. They're just sort of a grid system dividing the fields into regular square-mile sections. We hummed along on the crown of the straight road, and I managed to half forget The Ghost of Deckers' Cabin.

The radio was crooning old tunes again, and we were sitting closer together. He might even have thrown one arm around me if he'd been that kind of a driver. After driving up one road and down another for awhile, we saw the lights of an oncoming car far on in the distance. It was coming up fast, so Jerry eased off the crown of the road to give it plenty of room. The lights got brighter, and Jerry flashed his dimmers down, then up, then down again. But there was no response from the other car. It came dead on, and the lights flooded our whole windshield with a white glare.

You can't judge distances blinded like that. Before I realized it, the car's headlights were practically matched up with ours. They couldn't be more than a few yards away. It happened in a second, but it was like slow motion. I could feel my mouth opening, but no sound came out.

In that last second, Jerry veered to the right, and the oncoming car jumped away from us. He fought the wheel a little as we hit the soft shoulder, and I heard a scream from the other car. Not a scream like the one I was trying to get out. It was a screech of laughter—female laughter. Like a crazy banshee.

We ran along the shoulder for awhile. Jerry had the sense not to jerk back onto the blacktop. When we slowed down enough, we bumped easily back up on the road. His timing was right. A few yards farther along, there was a concrete culvert over a drainage ditch instead of the earth shoulder.

Jerry seemed calm enough, but his voice had a tight sound when he said, "Somebody's playing games with us." I didn't trust my voice to say anything.

When we came to a turnoff, Jerry pulled over and stopped the car. I didn't know what he had in mind, but when he got out, so did I. I thought he might be checking for damage, but he went around and stood up on the big, wooden, front bumper. He was looking back over the Plymouth in the direction the other car was taking. We could just see red taillights in the distance.

Then it came to a corner, turned right, and we could watch it way off in the dark by following the beams of its headlights. It was really moving.

Jerry said, "They're probably going to make a square and head back to town. We'll most likely meet them if we go straight ahead to the next corner and turn left."

Before I could react to this terrorizing plan, he was back in the car. As we roared off, he said, "Reach in the glove compartment and get out that big flashlight. See if my shades are in there, too." I handed over the flashlight and a pair of sunglasses. We turned left at the next corner. In a few seconds, sure enough, headlights loomed up ahead of us. History was about to repeat itself.

Jerry hooked the sunglasses over his ears in one swift gesture and flipped the sun visor down over the upper part of the windshield. He had the flashlight—a big, heavy-duty one—ready in his right hand and was steering with the left.

As the headlights of the oncoming car began to slant over to our side of the road again, I could tell that, though I was blinded, Jerry wasn't. The two cars headed straight at each other. I had my hands braced against the dashboard, for all the good that would do me. At the last moment, we were forced off the road, almost as before, hitting the earth with a sickening slither. But there was one difference. Just as the other car pulled past, Jerry shone the flashlight full in the eyes of the other driver. It happened in a split second, and then Jerry dropped the flashlight into his lap and used both hands to control the car. He'd lost a second though, and the shoulder was softer.

Again, he couldn't risk cutting the wheels to swerve back up. The loose dirt kept dragging us farther over. "Easy, easy, easy," Jerry was saying in a whispering chant, but whether he was talking to himself, or to his car, or to me, I couldn't tell.

I wish I could say that's all I remember, but my brain recorded everything. The Plymouth bounced and rocketed along out of control, and we were heeling farther and farther over. I thought the rollbar was about to have its first road test. Then there was a strange, unearthly scraping sound like a thousand twanging fiddles tuning up. My head hit the ceiling, and I came down again, sprawling half out of the seat.

There was a spooky stillness. It took me a moment to realize that we'd stopped. In that moment, Jerry had flipped off the ignition. My first impulse was to get out, but though the door on my side would unlatch, it wouldn't swing open. We'd come to rest against a woven-wire fence. A couple of fence posts were out of the ground behind us, but we'd kept from turning over by being jammed against the wire of the fencing. It was holding my door shut.

Jerry could get his door open about halfway before it dug into the lower bank of the shoulder. We'd dropped down a good three or four feet, plenty steep enough to have flipped us several times. He took hold of my wrist and pulled me across the seat and out. Then he started to turn to check the damage on the Plymouth, but scrambled up onto the road instead, pulling me along. We looked back down the road.

After all that wild motion, I nearly staggered and fell down on the solid blacktop. *We're alive.* That was the only fact I could absorb for the time being. Jerry dropped my hand and jumped back down in the ditch and came back with his flashlight. He aimed it back down the road. Then I saw it. It was the rear end of a car, sticking up at an odd angle, its hood out of sight in the opposite ditch. Jerry's plan had worked all right. He'd dazed the driver, who had lost control in that second of blindness. Those maniacs were finished with running people off the road. Then, I realized they might be finished completely. We both started running at the same time.

The car had swerved on and off the road for quite a distance. There were big S-shaped tire tracks of loose dirt on the blacktop. But finally, the car had shot off. We could hear steam hissing out of the radiator. One of the rear wheels was off the ground. Jerry flashed a light (for the second time) into the driver's seat. Somebody—a boy—was slumped over the steering wheel. It was bent nearly double under his weight.

Jerry reached under the wheel and turned off the ignition. The far door was open. There wasn't much hood left. What there was of it had wrapped around a fence post. The dead headlights were almost staring into each other's eyes. "Let's get him out," Jerry said. He handed me the flashlight and wrenched the bent door open. The inside of the car smelled like a brewery. There was blood all over the driver's face.

Jerry lifted him out with ease, and when he was stretched out on the road, he was a lot bigger than Jerry. He was also breathing.

"I think he's just got a bang on the head and some scalp cuts," Jerry said. "The windshield's in one piece, so he probably didn't crack his head too hard on it."

When I saw we didn't have an unidentified corpse on our hands, I was able to remember something else. It skittered around my mind a minute before I could zero in on it. It was that laugh. That girl's shriek of a laugh the first time the car had headed at us.

I looked again at the door on the opposite side, which was hanging open. "Jerry, he wasn't alone." We ran around the back of the car, and I aimed the flashlight down.

There were a few inches of black ditch water looking cold and nasty. I was hoping I was wrong, hoping there wasn't going to be anybody down in that black water.

But there was. A girl was lying about six feet from the car. The flashlight found her feet first, and I nearly dropped it. But then we heard a blurred squawk of a voice just as the beam hit her face.

"For cripe's sake, get that light outta my eyes."

It was Mitsy Decker.

10 | It took both of us, but we got Mitsy up out of her watery resting place. She was fighting drunk and took a couple of swings at Jerry, missing him a mile. She could barely stand up. And didn't know me from Adam, not that she would have cold sober. Jerry whispered for me to keep her from going around to the other side of the car where her boy friend's gory head might send her into hysterics.

She was wild enough as she was and kept muttering, "Lissen, I been around. I know!" But what she knew she wasn't able to say. I tried getting her to sit down on the road and hush up, but she was hauling off to deliver a powerhouse left hook to the side of my head. It was possible that her aim was improving, so I moved out of her range, and she lurched around the car just as the driver was sitting up. Jerry was kneeling down beside him with the flashlight, and Mitsy could see his face. The boy was mopping his forehead with a handkerchief and shaking all over. "Who is he, Mitsy?" Jerry asked.

She looked at him like she'd never laid eyes on him in her life. Then in a furry, faraway voice she said, "Some guy. I forget his name. Met him at MacDonald's. I can't think. Something must of happened."

"Yeah," Jerry said, "something sure did."

"Did we have a wreck?" Mitsy asked, trying to focus on the car. "We couldn't of. He's an exp . . . an exp . . . a good driver." I was beginning to think Mitsy must have landed on her head.

"Yeah," Jerry said, "he's one great driver."

Jerry sent me back to his car for a blanket out of the trunk. Then he told me to find the nearest farmhouse and ask them to call the sheriff.

I ran up a lane where I could see a faint, bluish glow from a house at the end of it. A farmer and his wife were watching TV when I pounded on their door. Luckily, they were a cool-headed pair. He made the call and told his wife he'd take the truck down to where the accident was. When I started to follow him out, the woman said, "No, you don't, honey, you're staying with me." My teeth were chattering, and I felt chilled to the bone. "You're going to lay right down on that there davenport and have a hot cup of coffee. You're in shock."

I did as I was told, and she threw an afghan over me. Suddenly, I was so tired I couldn't move my little finger. She held the coffee cup while I drank.

It was a lifesaver. When I was calmed down enough, she said, "Your folks know where you're at?"

"My gosh," I said, sitting bolt upright. "What time is it?"

"About time for the eleven o'clock news."

"My mom won't be home yet. She works nights and doesn't get home till after eleven-thirty."

"Well, she'll have to know, won't she? You

won't get home ahead of her." She was a pretty shrewd woman.

Mom would have to know, all right. There wasn't any question about that. "Go ahead and watch the news if you'd like to," I said.

"Never mind about that. You're about all the news I need for one night. How about another cup of coffee—and this time *you* hold the cup."

It was midnight before I had a chance to call Mom, from the phone booth in the emergency ward of the hospital. The sheriff insisted on taking us all there. They decided to keep Mitsy and her boy friend overnight for observation. Getting to the bottom of the accident was obviously going to be a long and involved business. One thing was clear though. Jerry and I were sober, while the other two weren't.

Mitsy was howling the place down and screaming, "Dumb fuzz!" over and over at the top of her lungs. The sheriff told a deputy to take Jerry and me home. As we drove away, I saw the Deckers' Dodge drive into the hospital driveway.

The police car waited at the curb while Jerry walked me up to our house. Mom was standing in her old wrapper on the top step, looking like doom. She never gave Jerry a glance. "Mrs. Patterson—" he began, but she just looked straight at me and said, "Inside."

She banged the door in Jerry's face and turned on me. "Well, you've made quite a night of it for a girl who was just going to stroll down and have a look at the bonfire." You could cut the sarcasm with a knife.

"Mom, listen—"

"Listen nothing! Get up and into bed. I'll deal

98

with you tomorrow, but I'm going to give you one thing to think about, and I want you to think about it good and hard. I've had enough trouble with Ellen to last me a lifetime. I'm not going to have any trouble with you! Do you hear me, young lady?"

I heard her all right. Every word.

The next morning was Saturday. For a couple of painless minutes after waking up, I didn't remember what had happened. They passed in a flash. I looked over, dreading to find Liz bright-eyed and ready to hear everything, but she was gone and her bed was made. I was hoping Mom wasn't up yet. I needed a few minutes to pull myself together—actually a few hours would have been more like it. I was worried about Jerry, about the car, about how I could explain it all so Mom would understand. Maybe I could make her listen.

I knew she felt that Ellen's trouble was partly her fault, that she hadn't ever really had any control over her. Now this had to happen to me. I'd probably be under house arrest for years. That was depressing enough, but what really made me sick was not being trusted. I hate not being trusted.

I thought things couldn't look worse. I was wrong.

The front doorbell rang. Mom answered it right away, which meant she was already downstairs and dressed. Whoever it was, it gave me a few more minutes. I started getting dressed and taking my time about it.

Just as I was pulling a sweat shirt over my head, Mom yelled from the foot of the stairs,

"Carol, come down here on the double!" As I started down, she was shooing Liz out the front door. A distinctly bad sign. Mom jerked her head toward the living room, and I followed her in.

There was a big, red-faced woman in a fur-trimmed coat sitting there. "This is my daughter, Mrs. Decker," Mom said in a very businesslike tone.

That about knocked me out. Any chance of having a reasonable talk with Mom was lost. But all I could do was face this. "Hello, Mrs. Decker. How's Mitsy?"

Mrs. Decker drew herself up and clutched her pocketbook with ten bright-red claws. "She's about as well as can be expected. We're going to bring her home from the hospital this afternoon after the doctor has another look at her." There was a tone in her voice that made it sound as if the whole thing had been specially arranged as a personal insult to her.

She gave Mom a quick look and said to me, "To be frank, I couldn't get anything very sensible out of Mitsy when I saw her this morning, and I thought perhaps you might be able to tell me just exactly what happened last night." She cleared her throat with a nervous little cough. I was glad she was making herself uncomfortable, too.

I opened my mouth to start telling her, but she wasn't finished. "I understand that you and my daughter and, ah, two boys were out at our cabin last night before the accident."

"Then you understand wrong," I said quickly.

"Carol!" Mom started out of her chair. "You

watch that mouth of yours. You're in enough trouble as it is!"

I realized then that every word I said was sure to get me in deeper and deeper. So I just sat there. But they were going to wait me out. So I had to try again. "After the bonfire last night, I was out riding in the country with a boy named Jerry Rodebaugh. The car—"

"Wait just a minute, young lady," Mom said. "A boy picked you up at the bonfire, and you went tearing out around the countryside with him?"

"No, Mom, he didn't pick me up. We had a date."

"That's funny," Mom said in a very unfunny voice. "I don't remember giving you permission to go out on a date. I don't believe I even know the boy. Did you have my permission? Maybe it just slipped my mind."

Boy, how I hate sarcasm. "No, Mom, I didn't ask you if I could. I just went." More silence. The air was getting heavier by the minute.

"Mrs. Patterson, perhaps if we could just let your daughter tell what happened." Mitsy's mother was on the verge of losing control of the conversation, and she knew it.

"We were out driving and a car came down the road, headed straight for us, ran us off into a ditch, and then it went out of control and drove off the other side of the road and piled up. We got out of our car and went back and found Mitsy and the boy who was driving the other car. Mitsy was in the ditch, and the boy was behind the wheel."

After training her eyes on me awhile, Mrs. Decker said, "Yes, well, that's no more than I

101

know already. And it's a good deal less than I suspect. Are you sure there's not more you can tell me?" Our cramped little living room was beginning to seem more and more like Traffic Court.

"No, that's not all," I said. "Mitsy was drunk out of her mind, and I suppose the boy driving was, too. He'd have to be to drive like that. He nearly killed all of us."

I was surprised that I got that much of a speech out before one or the other of them jumped on me. But Mom said in a fairly calm voice, "Carol, how can you be so sure they were drunk? That's a serious accusation."

I told them how I was so sure: the smell in the car, the way Mitsy was acting. Besides that, I knew the Deckers had come to the hospital while Mitsy was still carrying on. Mrs. Decker didn't need me for proof there. She was shifting in her chair.

"Yes, well, never mind that," she said. "There's something else I'd like to get to the bottom of. Mitsy says that the four of you were at the cottage. Do you deny that?"

"We weren't at the cottage together." Mrs. Decker obviously didn't choose to believe that.

"Mitsy knows I don't want her out there alone with a boy. I certainly don't want her out there under any circumstances, but the fact remains, she says the four of you were together. I know there's no safety in numbers, but I want the truth, and I'm going to have it."

I began to see Mitsy's game. She must have let it slip that she and that guy were at the cottage, and she wanted to share the blame.

She knew Jerry and I had driven out and were parked nearby, so that's all she needed.

Maybe, just maybe, I could have explained to Mom that Jerry and I drove out to the lake and parked for ten minutes and came back. And maybe she would understand, but not with Mrs. Decker sitting there, cross-examining me.

"Mrs. Decker, Mitsy's not a friend of mine. We don't double-date. We don't even speak. She's a friend of my sister, not me." It seemed pretty good as I was saying it. I thought it even sounded dignified. But, of course, it was exactly the wrong thing, as usual.

"Yes," Mrs. Decker said with a sneer in her voice. "I know all about your sister."

"Now wait a minute," Mom said. But Mrs. Decker wasn't waiting for anybody.

"I know all about your sister, and I'm very sorry to hear that my daughter ever had anything to do with her, and furthermore, I seriously doubt that she did. Mitsy is a high-spirited girl, but we have never had any trouble with her until last night. And certainly she's not the kind of girl to have Ellen's, ah, trouble."

She was aiming her guns at Mom now, which meant she was a more stupid woman than I thought. "Mr. Decker and I have exercised every control over our daughter, and we have always been very particular about the friends she has. A girl like Ellen—a *promiscuous* girl—is precisely the sort we have been glad she has never associated with."

There was a very small part of me that wanted to burst out laughing, even though this was no laughing matter. Mrs. Decker had puffed herself up to gigantic proportions with this grand speech and there was another pause.

Broken by Mom: "Get out of my house."

"Now see here," Mrs. Decker began. That's the way she ended, too. Mom was out of her chair and had Mrs. Decker by the upper arm. She quick-marched her to the front door, shoved her through it, and slammed it behind her. I never moved, wondering where we stood now.

We didn't stand together, I'm sorry to say. I had time to hope we would while Mom stayed at the front door, with her forehead pressed against the glass panel, trying to get hold of herself. There was a slim chance that Mrs. Decker's attack could bring Mom and me together.

But when she came back in the room, she was determined to start all over—on her terms. I noticed silly, pointless things. How orange Mom's dyed hair looked when her face was that white. How pinched her mouth was, even worse than it had been ever since Ellen left.

"All right," she said, "let's hear it again. All of it." I guess it's the only way we can communicate. She barks a command to her trained dog, and I can't ever jump high enough to suit her. But I tried. I started with the bonfire, but that wasn't good enough.

"I want to know how you met the boy in the first place."

I told her that. It didn't satisfy her. There was a question behind her eyes, like she was trying to sift out one droplet of truth from a whole ocean of lies. And I wasn't telling lies.

It took the rest of the morning, but I got the whole story told. About driving down to the

104

lake, seeing the cabin door start to open, how Mitsy and her boy friend took out after us, mean and drunk. How they tried to get us twice.

When I came to the part about the flashlight, Mom stopped looking skeptical for a couple of minutes and just looked plain fascinated. I told her everything. I hoped she'd be glad enough I wasn't hurt to soften up a little.

But when I finished, all she said was, "Are you sure nothing happened when you parked out by the lake?"

What did it matter that I was sure? She never would be.

11 | It was a week before the letter came—a week of being watched. Mom was really making up for lost time with Ellen at my expense. She managed to call Jerry all the names she wished she'd called Kevin. Not that she was ever liable to know either of them. To tell you the truth, I think after a while she began to think Jerry *was* Kevin. When she'd start on him, tears would come in my eyes, burning hot, but I'd hold them back. I wouldn't give her the satisfaction.

She watched me all she could. She'd even call in the evening from work. Sometimes, two or three times a night, depending on how busy she was. When Liz would answer, that wasn't good enough. I'd have to come to the phone. She thought Liz might be covering for me. And Liz would, too, but I'd never ask her.

Those calls were always the same:

"You at home?"

"Yes."

"Alone?"

"No. Liz is here."

"You know what I mean. Stay there. I might call again."

"I know."

That was it. You could hear the sounds of The Pull-Off Plaza in the background—dishes and trays clattering, the rumble of people's voices, piped-in music. Then the dial tone.

On Monday, I saw Jerry at lunch time. I think he made a special trip to school just to see me. I was counting on it. But earlier, during first period, two girls everybody refers to as Myrna-and-Marcia, because they're inseparable, swooped down on me at my desk. They'd never so much as passed the time of day before. I couldn't believe they were favoring me with their attention.

"Big time Friday night," one or the other of them said, with kind of a glassy-eyed leer.

This sudden attention caught me completely offguard. "I don't know," I said. "I didn't stay around for the dance."

"Don't we know it!" they said, more or less in unison, exploding into shrieking giggles.

That was the morning I stopped feeling invisible.

Jerry was waiting for me outside the cafeteria door. He turned me around by the elbow, and we started off down the hall. "Let's go across the street." Which meant Mickey's Place. It's the smokers' alternative to the school cafeteria and generally considered a low dive.

I'd never been in it, but the outside looks like the remains of a livery stable in a Grade B western. Inside, it's dark, loud, smoky, and jammed.

A voice out of the crowd yelled, "Hey, Jerry, how's the car?"

He maneuvered me back to an empty booth behind the jukebox. Since this was no place for my sack lunch, I shoved it down into the darkest corner of the seat. "Well, how is it?" I asked him.

"The car? Not much paint on your side."

"I'm not surprised about that. But you'll take care of it."

"Already started. I got it pretty well sanded down this weekend. Think I'll spray-paint it myself. She was beginning to pucker a little along the stripping anyhow. Might even dude her up with a racing stripe. What's your favorite color?"

Just then a big, blonde woman with a couple of buttons missing off her waitress uniform came up. She had one of those outsized handkerchiefs with multicolored crocheting on it pinned up on her shoulder. "Hey, Jerry—King of the Road—what'll it be?"

"Hey, Cleo, knock it off."

"Oh, I hear everything! Isn't anything I don't hear!" Cleo boomed out, ignoring me altogether. "What are you doing in here this time of day? Don't tell me you took a notion to attend high school for a change!"

"Cleo . . . you 'bout ready to take our orders?"

"Sure, Hot Rod, any old time."

When she was finally gone, we just sat there. Jerry looked neat and slicked up, like this was another date, which it was in a way. Except for his fingernails, which had permanent half-moons of black grease, he looked too neat for school. Starchy white shirt that glowed in the dimness of Mickey's Place. Cuffs turned carefully back and a comb sticking out of the pocket. Hair all in place and out of his eyes. You couldn't really picture him walking back across the street to class.

The easy part of the conversation was over. Somebody fed the jukebox, so it was throbbing right against my back. He said something too low to hear.

"What?"

"I said is your Mom still pretty mad?"

"Worse than that."

Jerry's black-edged nails drummed on the table top in time to the music for a while. I don't know what I expected him to say or do. It was all so hopeless. It wasn't even as if I was his girl or anything. One date doesn't really mean anything, and I couldn't expect him to stay interested considering the mess things were in. I wasn't even sure I *wanted* him to stay interested. There didn't seem much future in it.

The big waitress came back with hamburgers, cokes, a greasy paper of French fries—and more friendly chatter for Jerry. I felt like telling her she was old enough to be his mother, but I was pretty sure she'd have a comeback I wouldn't want to hear.

The food gave us something to do, even if I couldn't taste it. Part way through the hamburger, I started to wonder if he was picking up the check. I hoped so because I was as broke as usual.

"You want to take a walk or something after school?" he said. "I don't have to go to work till six."

"No. Mom expects me home right after school. She thinks you and I—"

"Yeah, well." The blond hair fell over his fore-

109

head as he carefully folded up the French fries'
paper into the smallest square possible.

"Well," he said finally, "I guess you wouldn't
want to bug out of school this afternoon. We
could go down to the garage and have a look
at the car or something."

It was getting clearer by the minute that he
was just filling in time. I didn't know which one
of us I felt sorrier for. "I guess I'm in enough
trouble without skipping school," I said. "Anyway, we'd just get caught. You don't get away
with much in this town."

It was true enough, what I said, but there
was more to it than that. I wouldn't have skipped
school to be with Jerry anyway. Not that I knew
what it was I was going to school for. But it was
something. At least, Jerry cut because he was
more interested in his car and things like that.
I couldn't think of anything in the world at that
moment that was of the slightest interest to
me. I don't know. I was all mixed up. The music
didn't help either. It just kept pounding away.
The smoke stung my eyes. All I wanted was to
get away. Away from Jerry even.

Finally, the waitress came back with the check
and a big smirk. "Put it on my bill, Cleo," Jerry
said, looking up with a grin like he was relieved
to talk to somebody besides me.

"You got to be kidding!" Cleo said and tried
to ruffle up his hair, which made him jerk his
head back.

"Well, if you insist." He pulled out a fairly
respectable wad of dollar bills and peeled off a
couple of them.

When we got outside, half blind from the
sunlight, the kids were streaming back into

school. "This is where we part company, I guess," Jerry said.

I was trying to feel miserable about whatever those words might mean, but most of all I just wanted to get back to school and be swallowed up by the thundering herd heading for fifth period.

"Well, thanks for lunch."

"Forget it. See you."

"Sure. See you."

It's impossible to figure some things out. The way Mom was breathing down my neck night and day, you'd have thought I'd hang on to Jerry like grim death just to spite her. But I wasn't even tempted. Don't think I was trying to be the obedient little daughter. She wouldn't have believed it anyway. But trying to go on with Jerry just wasn't the solution somehow. The way he was at Mickey's Place with Cleo, for example. It was like he sort of fitted in there and I didn't. Like in his own way, he was perfectly satisfied with life just as it is. I'm not. Maybe I never will be.

Apart from those required phone "conversations" with Mom, I drifted pretty quietly through the evenings of that week. Looking at homework assignments and letting my eyes drift off over the patterns on the oilcloth that covered the kitchen table. Green and black and white checks and some worn places where the canvas backing showed through. It was like a map of some dull country.

Liz hovered around, looking wise as usual, though willing enough to hear more. But I didn't feel like words. They never seem to work for me.

Then the night before the letter came, I was lying in bed trying to make my mind a complete blank and get to sleep with as few depressing thoughts as possible. I just about made it too. I was lying on my stomach with one hand trailing off down on the floor, which is always my final settling-in position. Then something soft brushed against my hand. Another minute or so, I'd have been asleep. As it was, I probably wouldn't have noticed it. But it happened again. Soft, furry feel, this time butting against the palm of my hand down on the floor.

I shot straight out of that bed and lit right in front of the light switch with visions of rodents whirling in my head. When I flicked on the overhead light and turned around, the first thing I saw was Liz, sitting up with crossed legs on her bed, as if she'd been that way all along instead of being asleep. Something peculiar was going on—no question about it.

"Say, I think there's something under my bed. Something alive." I hated to say the word *rat*, not so much because it would scare Liz, but because it would scare *me*.

Liz never moved. But something did. I'd pulled my sheet down half off onto the floor when I blasted off out of bed. The sheet twitched. Then, it twitched again. While I was watching it with eyes bulging out of my head, Liz just sat on her bed, watching me.

Then I heard a faint, scratching sound. The quietest little sound in the world, but definitely a sound. "I'm going for a broom. You stay put," I said to Liz.

"No, don't" she said.

So I didn't. Then from around the corner of the sheet a very small head appeared. A pair of yellow, almost glowing eyes with black centers looked right up into mine. And out strolled the most pathetic, ragged-looking gray cat you ever saw. There isn't much floor space to maneuver in so the cat looked around once and with an easy jump sailed up on my bed. It turned around twice, to make a nest for itself, but Liz's hands were outstretched, and it walked over to her instead, stepping daintily across the narrow gap between our beds.

"Poor Otis," Liz said in a soft, crooning voice. "Poor old Otis, how's your paw? Let me look at it." The cat—Otis—came within range of Liz and sat down, comfortably, circling himself with a tail that was missing quite a lot of fur. He licked one forepaw to wash his ears in a quick little circular motion. He wasn't in Liz's lap, but close enough to make them look like friends. Then he rolled over on his back, showing a fairly white throat, and invited Liz to stroke it.

She did, intently watching the cat and carefully not looking at me. When she had the cat half dazed with pleasure from the throat-stroking, she reached down and took hold of his right rear paw. There was a sore on the inner part of the leg, a little raw, pink place. All around it was slicked-down fur where the cat had been licking it. "It looks a little better, I think, Otis," Liz said in the same private, soft voice. She looked up at me and said, "I named him Otis."

I couldn't stand there watching all night. "Where in the world did that cat come from, Liz?"

"Sh. Hush. Don't wake Mom up. I've been very careful. Haven't we, Otis?" Otis jerked his sore paw away, but he stayed put.

"Now look, what is all this?"

"Well," she said, "I'm just looking after him till his paw gets better. He didn't have a home, so I brought him in. He didn't want to come at first, but now he likes it here." She was sitting on her bed with her legs crossed Indian style, and I noticed how long and skinny they were getting. The cat was stretched out right in front of her. It was funny how they sort of matched. Both of them long and kind of starved-looking.

"You know Mom won't stand for it. She'll carry on about not being able to have another mouth to feed."

"She won't need to know," Liz said. "Otis is very quiet. I think he understands."

"Now, Liz, she'll discover him first thing in the morning, so don't get your hopes up."

"Oh, I don't know. He's been here a week, and neither one of you noticed him. I keep him up here. Sometimes, at night, I let him out on the porch roof, but he comes right back."

"You don't mean to tell me that animal has been in here a week without me knowing it!"

"Sure. He's afraid of everybody except me. But when you're asleep, he comes out and walks all over you and looks at you." Her face wrinkled up into a grin, but she was worried that I might spoil things.

"How do you feed him?"

"I keep a saucer of milk and some scraps from the table behind the shoes in the closet. And I have papers down under Ellen's bed for you-know-what. I change them every day when nobody's around. Otis is very clean and refined. I'd like to get him real cat food but it's two cans for thirty-nine cents. But if I get some money, that's what I'm going to buy him."

Otis got up and walked back across the beds and butted his head very gently against my knee, then settled down and looked up at me through eyes that were little slits.

"See," Liz said, "he really likes you."

The trouble was, I liked him, too.

Seeing that Liz was anxious, I said, "Well, maybe Mom won't mind too much as long as he doesn't eat a lot."

She relaxed when she heard that, and then, in a whisper, said, "You know, Carol, I have thought maybe Mom did know he was up here. I mean when I told her I'd clean our room without her even telling me to, she gave me a look like she thought something was up, but she didn't say anything. I think maybe you were the only one who didn't know about Otis. It's easier to fool you than Mom."

"What do you mean by that?" I said out loud, and she said, "Shhh."

"Well, nowadays you go around not noticing anything very much. Like nothing is happening around you. That's one reason I kind of needed Otis."

What could I say to that? I wanted to tell her she was wrong, but she wasn't. So I said, "As soon as I'm sixteen, in the spring, I'm going to find a part-time job somewhere. Then we'll buy plenty of cat food for Otis."

She looked up at me, and her eyes were all shiny and big. I bent down and patted Otis on

115

the head. He then let out a good, healthy meow, and Liz said, "Shhhhh."

The next morning when I woke up, I saw cat hairs all over the blanket. Refined, Otis might be, but he had a problem with shedding. I felt like a fool for not discovering his traces before. When I hung my head upside down to look under the bed, there he was, curled up into a round ball, looking me straight in the eye.

Then downstairs, I found the envelope on the front hall table. Not a postcard this time—a letter, addressed in Ellen's large, unformed hand:

Dear Carol,

I thought I'd better drop you a line or two because I'm leaving the Home. Frankly, it's got me down. You'd have to see this place to believe it—though I hope you never do. Ha Ha. Like I said in the postcard, it's not too bad, but the atmosphere finally gets to you. We're not exactly locked up, but nobody wants to go anyplace looking like we do. So everywhere you turn—depressing pregnant girls, or as the maternity clothes ads say, "Ladies in Waiting." Brother! You should see them. I have to room with this girl who never shuts up. She swears she's secretly married, and it's all a big mistake her being here. She's about as married as the rest of us, but she just keeps on and on about it, trying to convince herself. I'm about ready to take out after her with a hammer. I'll spare you the rest of them. We're all in the same mess, not to mention the same shape, and misery definitely doesn't love company.

You remember Miss Hartman? She was the lady that came down to see us. Well, I went in and had a talk with her. Told her I was about to get stir crazy, and she was very nice about it. Seems they want the girls to stay here in the Home at least for a few weeks "to get acquainted" as she puts it. Then there's this plan for those that want out, to go and live with families.

It's like this, you can arrange to live in with a "cooperating family" and help with the housework and look after the kids and like that. The family gives you room and board and a little spending money. Frankly, it sounds like heaven to me, even the housework.

A couple of days later, Miss Hartman took me to visit this family, the Courtneys, one evening, when they were all home together. It's a nice place, and I'd have a room to myself. It's a doctor and his wife and two little kids. They've taken in lots of girls from the Home before, and I was so anxious they'd like me I didn't know what to do. Then, the next day, they called up Miss Hartman and told her I could come.

So I'm going to move over to their house this weekend and I'll stay with them till it's time to go to the hopsital. They'll take me when it's time and everything. So if you ever need to know where I'm at, like if I should get any mail or anything, here's the address:

Dr. and Mrs. Mark Courtney
1191 Pine Street
Evanston, Illinois

I don't know where I'll be after I leave there.
After I get out of the hospital and all. Don't look
for me to come home.

Luv,
Ellen

I read that letter half a dozen times before I
noticed she hadn't called me Maewest.

While Ellen was at the Home, I never had
written her a letter. Now that she was in a real
home, I still didn't plan to write. A letter
wouldn't bring her back to Claypitts. I didn't
have any good, persuasive reasons to offer.
Besides, it's too easy to throw a letter away
and forget it. I could imagine Ellen doing that.
Especially since it wasn't me she wanted to hear
from. It was Kevin the Convict. And I knew,
even if she didn't that she'd never hear from
him again.

So, it was then I decided I'd have to go up
there and see her myself. Not that I thought it
would do a bit of good, but I had to try it. Even
if she didn't particularly want to see me, I
wanted to see her. Just see how she was getting
along. See for myself.

Now there were several good, sound reasons
why this was out of the question: school . . .
fear . . . Mom . . . money. I started working
through each one of them in my mind. I tried to
discourage myself, but it didn't work.

It wouldn't hurt to pull a Jerry Rodebaugh
and cut a couple of days of school for once in
my life. What's two days out of a brilliant aca-
demic career?

And the fear? Well, that involved the mental
turmoil of getting up the nerve to sneak out

118

of the house without being missed until I was on the late bus to Chicago that makes The Pull-Off Plaza stop at eleven P.M. And spending the night on the bus, and being turned loose in the middle of Chicago, and trying to find Ellen in the middle of six million people, and probably getting completely lost and never being found again. That's fear.

And speaking of fear leads us to Mom. I couldn't tell her I was going. I'd have to leave her a note she wouldn't discover until I was on the bus. And then facing her when I got home—if I ever got home—come to think of it, fear and Mom weren't separate categories.

And money? Well, that was different. Right from the beginning, I think I knew how I'd take care of that.

12 | I didn't talk it over with myself—what I was planning to do. I just did it. And while I was walking across town to Franklin Street that becomes Route 7 when it gets out to the city limits, it dawned on me that this was a trip I'd been meaning to take all along. Of course, now I had a good reason. Nothing like money for a solid motive.

Route 7 doesn't connect up with the Interstate. It doesn't do much of anything except wind around the hills and hollows on the way to some little jerkwater place called Greenup where hardly anybody ever goes. Just two skinny lanes of cracked slab running between such dismal establishments as The Polar Ice and Frozen Food Locker; Artie's Farm-Fresh Vegetable Center; and finally, down in a dip in the road, The Route 7 Fixit Shop.

My heart didn't start pounding until the Fixit Shop sign loomed up. Parked right out in front was that same old open-bed truck, just like I knew it would be. In those surroundings, it looked downright elegant. All around it was a regular graveyard of car parts, stovepipe elbows, bedsprings. Whatever rusts was there, an acre of it at least. Just about the last place in town you'd look for loose money. And in the middle of it all was a trailer. It was up on concrete blocks and what hadn't rusted out on it looked

120

even worse. Somebody had once painted it robin's-egg blue on the sides and aluminum silver on the roof, but it was fast settling into the junk all around it.

When I got closer, I saw an old, abandoned toilet bowl planted with asters right next to the door. I decided it still wasn't too late to turn back. Then I decided it was. I figured he was inside. My father.

The door opened and a woman stepped right out on the concrete-block stoop. She pulled the door shut behind her. A big blonde in a cardigan sweater she held bunched up over a wash dress. I looked at her and did a doubletake. It was Cleo, the waitress at Mickey's Place.

My mind was spinning, but something was falling into place. "Whatcha want, kid?"

I wanted to run, that's what.

"I want so see my—Mr. Patterson."

"What about?"

"Business." I don't know how I found that word. I was scared of her, and she surely knew it.

"Business, is it? Better come on in then." She had that same big, booming voice, like she was taking lunch orders, except not nearly so friendly.

It wasn't a workshop inside, not this end of it anyway. It was where they lived, Cleo and— him. Dim and filthy and smelling like fried catfish. Hard to breathe. There was a bed with a grayish-pink chenille spread. Other stuff too— papers and junk and a floor lamp without a shade. I didn't want to look. For one terrible minute, I thought she and I were alone. But there was another room behind a curtain, muffling the sounds of a ball game on TV.

"Hey, *Mister* Patterson, lady to see you on business." She came down hard on the word *Mister*.

He pulled the curtain back and ducked in under it. It was him all right. He looked just like he had that day in the park, when was it? Going on three years ago. Even had on an old ball cap—probably the same one. And in the cramped little trailer room, he looked like a giant, a big, tired giant with hairs growing out of his ears.

He looked at me while Cleo looked at him. She was quicker than he was, you could tell, quicker to spot something. "What's on your mind?" he said.

"I'd like to talk to you. In private."

He looked closer at me, studied me. Finally, he said, "You Ellen?"

"No. I'm Carol."

He rubbed his chin with the back of his hand. After a long moment, he said, "Cleo, step out in the yard."

"Like hell," Cleo replied.

He was big, but she wasn't much smaller. You knew he wasn't going to pick her up and fling her out of the trailer. "Come on in the back room," he said to me and held the curtain back. Cleo didn't follow, but she stayed right there on the other side. I imagined I could hear her breathing.

"What's on your mind?" he said again and turned up the TV a little. It was on a workbench, heaped up with speakers and coils of wiring. There were a couple of office chairs, but we didn't sit down. He didn't know what to do with me, but he didn't look mad or anything. Every once in a while, he'd glance over at the curtain.

"I don't want to bother you, but—"

"It ain't any bother," he said, very low.

"But I need your help, and I don't have anybody else to go to and—"

"You in trouble?"

"No, not me. But I need—" I couldn't get it out. "—I need some money. I have to go away."

The curtain jerked back, and Cleo stormed into the room. "Oh no! OH NO YOU DON'T! That's just what I figured!" Her voice filled up the whole trailer. She took two steps over to me and gave my shoulders a shove. I sprawled backward into a skittering old chair with wheels on its feet. "Listen, girl, you listen to every word I say." Her voice drowned out the ball game. "I been expecting something like this right along. I'm not one bit surprised. I knew one or the other of you'd be down here with your hands out sooner or later. And I want you to get this into your head since I can see you don't know nuthin! Any money comes into this place, I bring it in. If he's got a dime, it'd be a wonder. I work for it all. I bring it in. I decide how it gets spent, what there is of it. And I don't owe you—any of you—a thing in the world, so you see how quick you can get out and don't let me see your face around here again!"

She was standing over me, red in the face, with her big hands on her big hips. I wanted out—you can believe it—but she was blocking the way, making sure I got the message.

"Okay, Cleo," he said, very tired-sounding. "You got that out of your system. Now shut up."

"Look!" she whirled around at him. "You don't talk to me that way! You're in no position to talk at all. You get this brat of yours out of here before I lose my temper!"

I was up and edging toward the curtain. If she'd gone on a couple of words longer, I'd have been through the curtain and out. I didn't make it. She turned around, and they both looked at me. "I'm sorry," I said to him. "I'm sorry for the trouble."

On the way back to Franklin Street. I wasn't running, but I wanted to. I'd forgotten about the money, about why I went, everything. Everything, that is, except Cleo towering over me, raving like a mad woman, trying to scare him and me at the same time. But it didn't really work—scaring me, I mean. It just made me sorry for him, sorry and ashamed. Why did I ever let myself in for that? If Mom knew I'd gone down there, she'd have my head. But if she knew how he had to live, maybe she'd pity him a little bit. Or maybe she'd be glad.

I hardly heard the rustle of dead leaves behind me. The old open-bed truck rolled up and stopped right next to the curb, just a little ahead. It was him. I couldn't keep on walking. So I went over to the door.

He just sat there behind the wheel, looking embarrassed. "That Cleo, she don't know everything," he said, not quite looking me square in the eye. He pulled out some folded-up bills from his shirt pocket and held them across to me. "Would twenty-five dollars help?"

"I don't—I better not," I said, staring down at the leaves in the gutter.

"Go on," he said, "you need it or you wouldn't get up the nerve to come to me about it. I can spare it. Go on and take it."

There it was, enough to get me to Chicago and back and then some, as far as I could calculate. That was the reason for all this, a bunch of dirty, crumpled-up bills. But I hadn't known what they'd cost. I didn't want them now, but not taking them would be worse—worse for him. He wanted me to know he had money to give me.

"Sure," he said as I reached out and took them. "You need the money, you take it. I gave you a couple of quarters once. Remember?"

I remembered the quarters all right. I nodded and stepped back from the truck. "It isn't for anything foolish," I said.

" 'Course not, I knew it wasn't. Well—" He was looking straight ahead as he slipped the truck into gear. It rattled off slowly down Franklin Street.

13 | Some people make a regular career of running away. I mean they start out at the age of four or five and get as far as the corner before they're apprehended and marched back to captivity. Then they work up gradually and sign on as cabin boys on tramp steamers, never returning to their ancestral homes till they are rich and leathery old sea captains. I even read the other day about this girl who stowed away on a jet plane. Locked herself in the rest room, and they didn't discover her until Mexico City.

But I've had absolutely no experience, I never even so much as packed an overnight bag before. Not that this was my main problem. At first, the main problem was that money. I folded it up—two tens and a five—and stuck it under my pillow case. And every night, I could feel it right under my head. The first night, I definitely decided to send it back. I shouldn't even want his money. I'd send it back, and maybe Cleo would find out. Then she'd know he did have money of his own after all. She'd see he could give it to anybody he wanted to. That'd show her. And I shouldn't have wanted anything enough to go to him for it in the first place. I definitely called the whole thing off and went to sleep.

And the next morning, I woke up with money

in my pillow and plans in my head, plans to use it. Overnight, it had become a reason for going. I'd been through enough to get it, that was for sure. And by Wednesday, I was ready to go. Wednesday night, on the late bus that leaves The Pull-Off Plaza at eleven. If I waited down between the cars in the parking lot and jumped on the bus at the last minute, Mom would never see me. I could buy my ticket after I got on. That part would be easy if I could do it at all.

On Wednesday morning, I told Shirley during Art. She was applying a few basic colors to what she said was shaping up as a still life, but the canvas was still in its early experimental stage, as it would be for some time. I just whispered that I was going and why as Mergenthaler was beginning to make her rounds. When I got it told, Shirley just nodded. She understood that I wanted somebody to know, somebody who wouldn't try to change my mind for me. Then Mergenthaler was behind us, and we were busy, silent artists, hard at work.

I planned to tell Liz at the last moment. No sense worrying her in advance. Besides, I didn't want Mom to think Liz was part of the plot. So when I was folding up my other dress into the small and battered suitcase we used to put our dolls in when we went on backyard picnics, I hoped Liz would come into the bedroom and find me at it. I killed time by wrapping my toothbrush in many separate layers of kleenex, but she didn't appear.

I had the note laid out on the bed. I'd written it in study hall for Liz to give to Mom. I checked under the bed, but Otis wasn't there. He had the run of the house in the evenings, when Mom wasn't there, of course. I waited as long as I could and then started down the stairs with the suitcase and the note. It was like walking The Last Mile. And the house seemed empty. Where was Liz?

She was in the living room, sound asleep in the big chair. Her skinny legs were under her, and a book, *The Little Prince,* had slipped out of her hands and was lying on the floor. Otis was curled up in her lap with his yellow eyes at half-mast. I started to wake her up, but instead I left the note on the arm of the chair. There was a minute or two before I had to leave. I stood over her, thinking she'd wake up on her own, but she was completely out, deep in dreamland, with Otis for security.

It reminded me of something way back, something I couldn't quite put my finger on at first. Then I remembered a part of our old rhyme, the one she'd outgrown;

> Old Black Cat down in the barn
> Keeping five small kittens warm
> Let the wind blow in the skies
> Dear Old Back Cat close your eyes.
> Little Child all tucked in bed
> Looking such a sleepy head
> Stars are quiet in the skies
> Little Child now close your eyes.

But hers were already closed. I walked out then, pulling the front door shut behind me, very carefully.

At first, the bus looked full. There were little dim lights along the ceiling, but they didn't help much. Then part way back I saw there was about half a seat next to a big fat lady. But the lights went out as the bus started to roll, and it was sit down or fall down. "Room here?" I asked her.

"Plenty!" she said. I eased in, and she tried to edge over. She was a heavy breather, and hot. Since it was late, almost everybody was settling down to sleep but her. She wore those glasses with little rhinestones in the frames, and they glittered. That was all I could tell about her face, but she was wide awake and ready to talk.

"Going all the way?" she asked. "Me, too. I'm going up to Hines Hospital." She pronounced it *hawspital*. "They've got my husband up there and can't do a thing for him. But it's a Veteran's Administration hospital so it don't cost him nothing. I'll never be able to bring him home. Couldn't look after him right if I did. They make him pretty comfortable. And there's activities. Jigsaws and lathes and like that in the occupational therapy. It's too much like the doggone army, though, is what he says. He hated the army, and I always tell him reason was because that's where he met me. You wouldn't remember, but they had such a thing as canteens during the war, and us girls, we used to go down and serve coffee and doughnuts and like that. Danced some with them. Wouldn't know it to look at me now, but during the war I could get into a size eight dress, ten really, but I liked a good fit. And you can take it or leave it, but I got fifteen or twenty proposals of marriage!"

She gave me a good healthy nudge with her elbow that was already wedged into my side. "Yessir. 'Course they didn't all mean it. They was all of them lonely and going overseas. The opportunities I had and I picked you, I always tell my husband, just pulling his leg, of course. He just snorts and it don't faze him.

"Well, sir, one night him and me were dancing—jitterbugging—and everybody just stood back in a circle and watched. Then right after that he said to me, if I get through this war, I'm coming back for you. You do that, I told him, like I told all the others. I give him my address. They always liked to have somebody to write to. I got so many letters during the war from different ones. I never have had anything like that much mail since. Well, anyhow, when he knocked on the door, I didn't know him from Adam. Didn't even remember his name. Didn't stop him though. We was married in six weeks, and we had our twenty-fifth silver wedding anniversary before he took sick. He won't be able to get out of the hospital though, and it's hard for me to get up to see him. A nine-hour trip each way. I could take him out in a car for a ride up there, but, of course, I haven't got one. Where you going?"

"I'm going up to see my sister."

"She married or working?"

"Working. She lives with a family."

"Well, that's better than alone, isn't it? She be glad to see you. You going to stay up there with her for awhile?"

Falling into a long, personal discussion with the first stranger I met hadn't exactly been my idea of running off in the dark of night. I appreciated it, though, since we were getting closer to Chicago every minute. And alone, I'd have panicked.

"I can't stay up there too long," I told her. "I go to high school. But I just wanted to see how she's getting along."

"Don't she write?"

"Well, yes, but—" Then it all came out. I told the fat lady in the rhinestone glasses everything. It was surprising what a good listener she was. And everybody around us was quiet. Asleep or eavesdropping, but it didn't matter. We were all strangers.

I finished up by telling her I was going to try to get Ellen to come home after the baby was born, that was why I was going up to see her. The lady was quiet a moment, thinking. "Be hard for her to give her baby up." I didn't say anything. "Be hard for her to keep it, though. These things happen. I have a sister, went out east and married a man out there, lives in East Orange, New Jersey. Says she wouldn't come back out here to live again for any money. Different situation, of course. A girl like your sister, though, makes one mistake and thinks the world's come to an end. It's pride, and it passes off. She'll come home when it's over and she can think straight. Happens all the time." She was quiet again for a little while.

"She's lucky, having somebody who cares, like you. That counts for plenty. It'll all work out, you'll see. Rest stop's at Watseka. You won't bother me any if you want to get out and stretch your legs. Me, I need my beauty sleep."

Then she took off her glinty glasses and put them in her purse. "Can't see with 'em and can't

131

see without 'em." And right away she was snoring.

It was daylight as we drove into Chicago. People were stirring and beginning to pull their coats down from the overhead rack. After a glance or two, I tried not to look out the window. I knew it would be big, but nothing like this. There was a panic bubble in my throat. I was scared to swallow for fear I'd break it. When we began to stop for traffic lights though, I couldn't keep from looking. You couldn't see to the tops of the buildings, but people were surging all around the bus, thousands of them. It was the morning rush hour, of course, but I didn't think of that at the time.

The fat lady woke up and began wiping off her face with one of those little presoaked tissues that come in an envelope. Then she planted the rhinestone glasses on her nose and glanced out the window. "Well, that's Chicago. Everybody stampeding first one direction and then another. Catch me living here! Know where you're headed when you get out of the station?"

I didn't trust my voice to speak, so I just shook my head. With a little encouragement, I'd have grabbed her hand. For once in my life, I could have used a little mothering.

I stuck by her while we collected our suitcases and all the way through the bus station. There was an escalator that led up to the street level and people lined up to get on it. When it came my turn, I couldn't quite arrange to get myself and the suitcase on the same step. So somehow I got on backwards and rode all the way up staring straight into the eyes of a tall man behind me. But I was too numb to know what I was doing.

Outside, you couldn't see the sidewalk for the people, and they were really moving—all in one direction. The fat lady and I were swept along. I fished out the address and showed it to her. "That's the northern suburbs," she said. "You and me both take the El, but I go west. We'll go on to the station together, though, and I'll start you out in the right direction."

It wasn't far. I heard the rumbling overhead and saw the tracks running way above the street, making it sort of evening underneath. A train was just pulling in as we started up the steps. It made everything shake, not that I wasn't shaking anyway. On the platform, the fat lady marched right up to a group of people. "This girl here wants to go to Evanston." She took the address out of my hand and showed it to them, while I stood there tongue-tied. They told me to get on the next train and ride to the end of the line and change over to the Evanston car. If they'd told me to jump in front of the next train that came in, I'd probably have done it. Gladly.

"You'll be all right," the fat lady said, her voice getting louder because a train was roaring in so close I thought it would blow us off the platform. "You're headed right anyhow. My train's over on the other side, so I'll say good-bye to you. And good luck in your endeavors." As she walked away, I realized I hadn't even been able to say good-bye to her, but I think she must have understood. Then the doors of the train jumped back, and I was pushed in with my suitcase banging my knees.

There was one empty seat, and I fell into it. A man came right up and stood over me, hanging onto a hook from the ceiling. He had to lean forward because my suitcase was where his feet should have been. But he didn't seem to notice. He held a big thick newspaper all carefully folded in one hand and never looked away from it.

I couldn't see much but the front of his coat, but it seemed like we were going fast enough to jump the tracks. On curves, everybody swayed, and there was a screaming, metal sound from the wheels. Wherever we were going, we ought to be there right away.

I rode to the end of the line and took the other train and kept showing people the address, like the fat lady did. Finally, I was walking down a nice, quiet street with the sound of the El train still ringing in my ears. My head buzzed with all the motion and a sleepless night. And the handle on the suitcase was cutting into my hand.

It was a pretty street, not fancy, but pleasant looking. Big, old houses and little kids out on tricycles and tall trees, arching bare branches over the sidewalk. I was too tired to think by then. When I came to the house with the number written on the paper, I stumbled up the walk and rang the front doorbell. Wherever I was, I couldn't go another step.

14 | The door seemed to be opening by itself. Then I looked down into a face a little lower than the doorknob. At least, it was something like a face. A nose three inches long with a large purple wart on it. Two big Bugs Bunny teeth attached to a red grinning mouth. A witch's hat over this and a sheet below it, dragging on the floor of the hallway behind. "Boo," it said.

"Boo yourself. Halloween's over."

The voice coming from behind the mask was muffled but clear: "No, it isn't, either. It's coming again. Do you want Mommy? She's probably in the bathroom on the—"

"No, she isn't. She's right here," came another voice from behind. "Excuse my daughter. She swears Halloween lasts at least until we put the Christmas tree up." The witch's mother stepped up, looking as pretty as a shampoo ad. She brightened up the whole hallway—and she was certainly wondering what a strange girl and a suitcase were doing on her front steps. As usual, I couldn't quite think where to begin.

"I came up on the bus. My name's Carol Patterson and—"

"Ellen's sister! I should have known you. Come right in. Ellen didn't tell me—"

"Ellen didn't know."

"Won't this be a surprise for her, Kristin?"

135

She reached down and swept off the hat and false face, and there was Kristin, staring up at me with big eyes. "Ellen's sister?" she said and then buried most of her face in her mother's skirt, keeping one eye uncovered and trained on me.

"Ellen's out shopping with our other monster, so the noise level's cut in half just now," Mrs. Courtney led me into a long living room furnished with big comfortable chairs and littered with toys. "So this is tea-break time. Will you drink a cup?" I nodded dumbly, still not quite believing I'd got where I was going. But I began to feel safe. Mrs. Courtney disappeared toward the kitchen. Kristin scooted after her, chanting, "10,9,8,7,6,5,4,3,2,1!"

Then Mrs. Courtney's head reappeared. "Don't think Kristin's confused about her numbers. She's learned them from the moonshot countdowns on television. It's going to come as a severe shock to her in first grade to learn she's been going backwards all this time." Then she vanished again, and I was left to settle deeper into a long, low sofa. I was just beginning to doze when Mrs. Courtney returned with a pot of tea and two cups on a tray, "Lemon or cream?"

My defenses were definitely down. "I don't know. I never had tea before."

"Cream, then. And plenty of sugar."

It brought me around. But I couldn't quite concentrate on what Mrs. Courtney was saying. She was just a pleasant sort of hazy impression on my fogged-up brain—pretty, young, and very nice. No demanding questions—like what I was doing out of school and whether or not Mom knew where I was—and no polite shock at having an uninvited guest. We drained the teapot, and she took the tray back to the kitchen.

This time, she was gone so long I really did drift off. I tried to keep awake by counting up the hours since I'd been to bed last, but that naturally had the opposite effect. When I came to, she was sitting in the chair across the coffee table from me again. In front of me was a large glass of orange juice, buttered toast, and a bowl of cereal. "It occurred to me that you must have missed breakfast."

When I'd eaten everything in sight, I said, "Ellen and I, we never were too close. You're probably wondering why I'm here at all."

"I expect you miss her and wonder about her. That's reason enough for any visit," she said. "I'll miss her myself when she leaves us. She's good company and a big help. And believe me, with two rascals and an overworked husband, I can use all the help I get. And we hope we're helping her, too. But we're only a substitute family. You're the real one."

I wondered if that's the way Ellen saw it.

"You'll find Ellen changed. For one thing, she's wearing some of my maternity clothes. But you'll probably notice more changes than that." Just then we both heard the front door open and a very shrill voice demanding a cookie. A small guided missile shot into the room, around the sofa, and straight into Mrs. Courtney's lap.

Trying to defend herself from this attack, she said, "This is Edward." Edward was a two-year-old fireball with red hair, red face, and red

137

corduroy overalls. He didn't look hungry, but he sure sounded hungry.

Standing behind me in the doorway was Ellen. I could sense her there. I began to tingle a little, but as I started to turn my head, she came around the sofa, not even noticing me at first, and said to Mrs. Courtney, "We stopped off at the playground, and the only earthly way I could get Eddy off the teeter-totter was to promise him a coo—"

Then, she saw me. We were close enough to touch. She started to clutch her coat around her. Her mouth was still moving on that sentence, but the words died out. "Carol?"

Even Edward was quiet. I don't think I've ever felt so shy in my whole miserable life. In the past half hour, Mrs. Courtney had made me feel like a friend, and now my own sister was like a stranger. We'd been strangers before, but never like this. It was true. She had changed—a lot. She was thick in the middle, heavy, in fact. She had on a smock under the coat she finally stopped trying to hide behind. Her hair was different. Longer and turned up at the ends—a lot like Mrs. Courtney's. Shiny and beautiful. She looked lots older. And she was puckering up to cry. Sometime along in there, Mrs. Courtney and Edward did a disappearing act.

I slept away most of that day in Ellen's room. It was big and airy, with a bath of its own, and a little winding stairway that led down to the kitchen. When I woke up, it was evening. There was a cozy, neighborhoody smell of burning leaves drifting in the window and voices from down in the kitchen. I lay there awhile,

138

remembering where I was, thinking how snug and comfortable it all was. Then I got up, put on my other dress, and started down the stairs.

I could hear a man's voice, so I was shy again. One minute at home, the next a stranger. But I couldn't stand on the stairs all night. The first person I saw was Dr. Courtney, with a towel wrapped around his waist for an apron. He was turning steaks on a broiler with a long-handled fork. Mrs. Courtney was washing salad greens at the sink, and Ellen was leaning over a small table where Kristin and Edward were having their supper. She was coaxing a carrot into Edward's mouth while Kristin waved her spoon over her head and supervised. It was like a picture of a family. No, it was better than that. It was the real thing. And Ellen fitted right in.

The dinner was the best I ever had. You can count on one hand the number of times I've had steak. But it wasn't just that. There were flowers in a brass bowl—curly chrysanthemums. And lighted candles that made the polished tabletop glow. Dr. Courtney could tell I was a little nervous. About him mostly. I mean, I know that's the way families are. Wife at one end of the table and husband at the other. But that's not the kind of life I've known anything about—except in books and looking through people's windows. But he got me talking somehow without me knowing how he did it. Pretty soon, I was telling them about Liz and her secret cat, Otis. It was something I could tell them about us that wouldn't sound completely depressing. Ellen listened too, I happened to notice.

But we all talked—real dinnertable conversation. Dr. Courtney told us about his day. About two of his patients—one lady who thought she was sick and wasn't, and another one who thought she wasn't but was. He made them sound like people not just cases. And Mrs. Courtney kept having to shoo a small witch in pajamas back to bed every once in a while.

Ellen wasn't quiet, either. She about made me swallow my fork in sheer shock when she started in on the price of groceries. Part of her job was doing the marketing. Ellen—who never knew what money meant and probably thought food grew in the refrigerator by itself. Right about then I began to see why Ellen wouldn't ever want to come home again. This was home.

They didn't treat her like a servant, either. We all helped clear the table, but Ellen and I did the dishes by ourselves. It was really our first time alone.

"Mom know where you are?"

"I left a note." (I was hoping she wouldn't ask where I got the money and, fortunately, she didn't.)

"That won't be enough for her. She'll have the National Guard out after you if you don't get in touch with her."

"I won't stay long."

"Oh, that part'll be okay by me. For a while, I didn't think I'd want anybody to see me. You know, looking like this." She stepped back from the sink, and we both gazed down at the bulge that made her apron stand out.

"Yes," I said in my considering voice, "you are beginning to resemble a kangaroo." She overlooked this observation.

"I didn't even want to go to the grocery store or take the kids out for a walk, but Mrs. Courtney just handed me my coat and headed me toward the door. So I got over that. She's wonderful—but she's firm. I hated the neighbors around here to see me, but she sat me down and reminded me that I wasn't the first pregnant girl they'd had come to live with them, and the neighbors didn't pay any attention anymore. This isn't Claypitts, thank God."

No, it wasn't Claypitts, sure enough. It was in my mind to point out to Ellen that Claypitts was where we lived, though. But maybe this wasn't the moment—or maybe, I was putting it off.

That night when we were in our beds in Ellen's room, I decided I'd better get started on her. After all, a whole day had gone by. I wanted to tackle her before I decided I couldn't stand going back home myself. Believe me, when you find out the world doesn't immediately swallow you up, you can begin to develop a taste for it.

But she had the first word (which isn't too different from the old days, by the way). She was winding her alarm clock and saying how she'd have to be up by seven to keep the kids out of the Courtneys' hair so they could have a peaceful breakfast. She wasn't complaining. She was just sort of mapping out her daily routine. The idea of Ellen playing the efficient Mary Poppins role was just about enough to blow my mind, even though I'd already watched her in action. If Mom could see her now! Or better yet —Liz.

"You know, Carol, what I said in the letter. I still mean it. If you've come all the way up here just to see me, fine. But if you're going to try to get me to come home . . . afterwards . . . well, I appreciate it, but save your breath. *Is that why you've come?*"

"Yes."

"Did Mom send you?"

"No. I told you I just left her a note and lit out. She wouldn't have let me." Ellen thought about that for a while. It made me wonder if she wished Mom *had* sent me.

Of course, nobody was particularly impressed that I'd made it all the way up here on my own (not counting the fat lady who put me on the El). Frankly, I thought that was quite an achievement, but I guess you have to be an unwed mother or something really spectacular to get any notice. It never was any use trying to get Ellen interested in anybody but herself. Some things don't change. So I tried again. "But what are you going to do? You can't stay here after the baby comes. You know that, don't you?"

"Of course I do." But there was something in her voice, something uncertain.

"Besides," I said, deciding I'd better press on, "you've got to finish school. Do you think you could get back in time for second semester? I mean, do you think maybe—" She was giving me this look. It was drying me up—fast. Then she rolled over on one elbow and really fixed me right in her sights.

"Now look, Carol, let's get one thing straight once and for all. Maybe I could get back for second semester, and maybe I couldn't. The doctor says it's the last week in January. But no matter what, I will not be going back to Claypitts High School next semester, or next fall, or ever."

"But—"

"But nothing. I'm not going back there where everybody knows everything about your business, and the only thing they have to do is snipe at you behind your back. I've had it with that whole crowd and that whole crummy town. How'd *you* like to have to face Mitsy Decker's sassy face if you were me?"

(Not to mention her mother, I thought privately.) But I said, "You mean you're too ashamed to go back and face them all."

"Okay, if that's what you want to think, think it. But just remember. You're not going through this. I am. Seems to me you ought to be able to understand it a little, anyway. Why should I want to go back there? What for? There's nothing there. Not for people like us. We're *losers*. Like Mom.

"And you want to know something? I'm almost glad this happened." She put her hand down under the sheet and patted her bulging stomach. "If it means I'm free of that Godforsaken place, I *am* glad!"

She flipped over on her back and stared at the ceiling. Just in case one or the other of us had somehow failed to get the message, she said it again: "I'm not going back. And nobody can make me do it."

I was willing to let this go as the last word on the subject for the time being. Frankly, Ellen wears me out. I slipped down farther under the covers and pulled the sheet up to my nose. After a little hesitation, she reached over and snapped off the light.

But I'd been asleep most of the day. I was wide-awake, now just when there was no point in it. Ten minutes or so passed. It seemed more like an hour.

"Ellen, you asleep?"

"No."

"Are you scared?"

"What about?"

"About when the baby comes. About having a baby."

"Yes," she said. I waited for more. But that's all she said.

15 | Maybe I heard the alarm go off at seven. I seem to remember deciding to rest my eyes a minute. When I got them pried open again, it was eight-thirty, and I had the room to myself.

By the time I made it down to the kitchen, Dr. Courtney was pouring himself a cup of coffee. Probably not his first one. He was dressed for work in a dark suit and a very subtle tie with a tiny red stripe in it. He was very handsome, and I felt another one of my attacks of withdrawal coming on. Before I go out into the Big World for keeps, remind me to take a mail-order course in poise.

Ellen, Kristin, and Mrs. Courtney were out burning the last of the leaves. So we had the kitchen to ourselves, except for Edward, who was sitting under the sink with one foot in a pan, humming a tuneless little song.

For a mature, woman-of-the-world touch, I decided to start off with black coffee. It was pretty clear that Dr. Courtney had been delaying his day to have a few words with me. It wasn't long before the conversation came around to Ellen. "So, Carol, how does she seem to you?"

"She's happy to be here. Anybody would be. What worries me is she may be too happy."

"You mean you're afraid Ellen's not going to want to go home?"

145

"She told you?"

"No. But it's usually that way. All girls in Ellen's situation have pretty much the same set of problems."

"But she'll have to, won't she? I mean she won't be eighteen till summer. She's always thought she was grown up, but she's not, yet."

"No, she still has a lot of growing up to do, more than you do probably. But you can't try to make other people's decisions for them, can you? I expect what Ellen's going through seems punishment enough to her without the added penalty of having to go home to face people there."

That was about it. In fact, it was really what Ellen had been saying the night before in her own way.

"She'll have to decide for herself, Carol." Dr. Courtney retrieved Edward from under the sink and sat back down at the table with him. It seemed that Edward, sitting there on his father's lap, fiddling with the coffee spoon, had something to do with the conversation, but I couldn't think just what. "Ellen's going to have a lot of ideas that may not make sense to anybody but herself in these months. She's feeling her way through a mess that seems to threaten her whole life. And she has her pride, Carol. Don't forget that."

I'd heard that before. But where? The fat lady on the bus, the lady in the middle of the night who had said, "It's pride, and it passes off."

"But she's liable to do something crazy, isn't she? I mean she can't manage on her own. She—"

"Who can't?" I splashed the rest of my coffee

into the saucer. Ellen was standing in the kitchen door, looking daggers at me. I don't think she'd heard more than that last sentence, but it was enough. "Listen," she said in a loud, quivery voice, "I thought I made it clear to you last night that—"

"Ellen, hold it right there. You'll traumatize Edward, coming on that strong." Dr. Courtney's voice was very calm, but it silenced her. For a moment.

Then, pretending to be calm herself, she said, "Carol, don't meddle. Just don't."

She had a point there, I guess. Meddling was about the size of it. Maybe I wanted Ellen home for reasons of my own. Maybe it was just an excuse, saying she couldn't look after herself. Maybe, maybe, maybe. Why wasn't anything certain? Would Ellen coming back home make us a family even when we hadn't been one before? No, that much was certain . . . maybe.

Dr. Courtney got up to leave for work—and suggested very strongly that we two have a nice, peaceful reunion and worry about the future later. I was willing, but time was short.

I gave myself two days, planning to leave Sunday to be back in school Monday, always assuming that Mom didn't hang me in chains the minute I stepped off the bus. So I kept my mouth shut and played it like a visit for the rest of Friday. Ellen was back to normal, more or less, but on her guard. She was waiting for me to start up again. In fact, she was so obviously waiting, I figured she'd make the next move. She did. But she took her time about it.

After lunch, Mrs. Courtney decided it would be a good idea to walk down by the lake, to

147

let me see it. So we bundled up the kids in their snowsuits because the day was winter-cold.

It was no light breeze that swept in off the lake. Except for us, the beach was completely deserted. The wind cut our eyes, but I'd never seen anything like the lake. In my limited experience, lakes are nothing but overgrown ponds. Lake Michigan is like an ocean. A long trail of smoke in the distance came from a ship below the horizon. And that great, gray stretch of water, pounding up on the beach in white waves. It was like the edge of the world—cold and clean and moody. There was even a light-house on a cliff above the beach, just like a painting.

We walked up by it, the kids scampering off constantly to pick up pebbles and throw them with mighty swings that sent them toppling over backward. Ellen kept them under control like a mother hen. It made me remember another thing the fat lady on the bus had said. "Be hard to give her baby up." And Edward, too. Edward sitting on his father's lap while we talked. Wonder why I didn't think of that as soon as I got to the Courtneys? Here Ellen was, looking after somebody else's children when all the time one of her own was growing inside her. But not one of her own, really. One to give away.

I guess there's something about gray water crashing up on an empty beach that gives you deep thoughts. I was drowning in mine.

It was late Saturday night before Ellen and I had a real, full-scale confrontation. The Courtneys had gone out to a party, and the kids had been put to bed often enough so they'd settled down at last. Ellen spent as much of the evening as she could fussing around the house. I was on the twitchy side, to say the least. In less than a day, I'd be back in Claypitts, facing the music for running off. And not a thing in the world to show for it.

When she ran out of busywork, we found ourselves just sitting on the living room sofa staring at each other. "Well," she said, "you've stopped meddling all right, but you're so quiet you're beginning to get on my nerves."

I added to the effect by saying nothing.

"But before you go, I'll tell you what I have in mind. Seems like you don't think I'm capable of making my own decisions. But there you're wrong. Maybe you won't fuss about me so much if you know I have a plan. Right?"

"Depends on the plan."

"Well, it's nothing absolutely definite. But I thought after the baby came—wow, will I be glad to be skinny again. Anyway, after it's over, I thought I'd finish high school up here. I can do that easy. You can go at night or take a course by mail. They advertise it on TV. There's lots of ways, Carol. Reason you don't know about them is you never were out of Claypitts before. Lots of things are possible."

Silence.

"Well, say something."

"What can I say?" I replied. "Since I was never out of Claypitts before, I'm too ignorant to know anything."

"Oh don't be so touchy. I'm just trying to tell you there are different ways of doing things."

"Well, all right then, how do you intend to live while you're up here finishing school?"

"I'll get me a job. I'll clerk in a store or something. These girls raised up here are all so rich they don't have to work. There's jobs going begging. I'll find something. I might even do some baby-sitting for the Courtneys now and then."

"I wouldn't count on that much if I were you. After you leave here, the Courtneys will get another girl from the Home. You know that."

"Maybe they won't get another one right away. You know they're particular about who they take. If you'd seen some of the losers that were in that Home with me before I came here! Some of them didn't have sense enough to come in out of the rain. I wouldn't trust them to look after a baby of mine! I nearly went crazy in that place before I got out. Some of them couldn't read or write! You can't imagine it. You haven't seen anything like it."

Maybe not, but one thing I *could* see without a bit of trouble was that Ellen would try to attach herself to the Courtneys' permanently if she could. So I told her so, and I also told her the Courtneys wouldn't stand for it.

"I know that," she said, "but there's no reason we can't go on being friends. I never had friends before, Carol. I never knew what friends were. They make me want to *be* something. You can see that, can't you?"

I could. But I couldn't see how it was getting us anywhere. So I tried another approach. "Where are you planning to live?"

"That depends. If I'm alone, I could live at the YWCA. It's cheap. There's one right around here, and there's plenty of them in Chicago. I looked them up in the phone book."

"Wait a minute," I said. "Hold on. What was that about *if* you're alone? Did I hear right?"

When she finally answered, her voice had a retreating sound to it, like she was slipping away from me, or trying to. "Don't forget, Carol, it's still my baby. I don't have to give it up unless I sign it away. They told me my rights at the Home before I came here. Nobody can make me give it up. Not unless I want to."

She could see how my eyes were bugging out, and it kept her talking—more desperately.

"That's the way it is. The natural mother has her rights. That Miss Hartman at the Home told us. We had group meetings about it. Some of the girls said they were going to give theirs up. Others said they were going to keep them. I didn't say. I haven't decided yet.

"Carol, they say if you're going to give your baby up, you shouldn't ever see it. I mean you oughtn't to look even to see if it's a boy or girl. If you don't really see it, it's easier not to keep it. That's what they said—don't look and it wont hurt.

"I don't know if I could keep from looking, Carol, unless I was unconscious or something."

She ran down then, and silence closed in. You could hear the clock ticking in the dining room and the wind in the trees.

What was it Dr. Courtney had said? Something about how Ellen would have ideas that didn't make any sense? But I wasn't prepared for this. I got up off that sofa and stood over her. She was trying hard to look responsible, but it wasn't coming off. She just looked lost.

151

And she was twisting her hands in what lap she had. It was right then that we got ourselves reversed. It happened right at that moment. I turned into the older sister—but, believe me, it didn't give me a bit of satisfaction. "That's crazy, Ellen, and you know it!" I tried to get her to look me in the eye, but she wasn't having any of that. "Get it out of your head. You've got trouble enough without having fantasies. You couldn't raise a child on your own and you wouldn't want to. You're only thinking about yourself! Your baby's got to have a real home and family, like this one. You can't give him that."

She tried to work herself up to give me a real blast in reply, but when she answered, it was only a whine—with a sob in it. And she'd apparently been saving back the wildest fantasy for last: "What if . . . what if Kevin got out and came looking for me? What then? What if he found out there was a baby and I'd given it away to strangers? It's mine. And it's his. What would he think of me then?"

"What did he ever think of you?" I said. Actually, I yelled it.

"He loved me."

"Did he tell you so?" She couldn't answer that. "He didn't have to tell you he loved you. He got what he wanted anyway!"

She looked up then. Oh yes, that got to her. "I hate you," she said. "I wish you'd leave here tonight. I hope I never lay eyes on you ever again." She started to get up, but the sofa was deep. She had to make two tries before she was even up on the edge. And she grunted. She was trying so hard to make a dramatic exit, but she was just a few weeks too pregnant to carry it off. I could give her one light shove, and she'd be right back where she started, I thought. Maybe her craziness was catching, but all at once I wanted to laugh. I wanted to laugh my head off.

And so I did. And I gave her a shove, too. Her head lolled back on the sofa, and she gave me this terrified look. Then she started to blubber. Then she started to laugh. Then I started to blubber. Pure hysteria, of course, but so what? We'd been through everything else.

By the time the Courtneys walked in on us, I don't know how long later, we'd both slid down on the floor and were laughing and crying and whooping and blowing our noses all over the place. And there stood the Courtneys, perplexed but interested.

What a mess we were. Me in my plaid Ellen-hand-me-down. She in Mrs. Courtney's old, hand-me-down maternity tent and both of us wet down the front from tears and crumpled up beyond repair.

And there stood the Courtneys over us. She in a little navy-blue number that fitted like a dream. And he, saying, "What have we here, a couple of nut cases?"

That sent us off again. We threw our arms around each other and screamed with enough damp laughter to wake up Kristin and Edward and every other sleeping child in town.

Finally, Ellen managed to gasp out, "We've got to stop this. I'll go into labor right now!" She stretched out flat on the rug, but it didn't really calm us down much. She looked like such a lump lying there.

She didn't go into labor that night, by the

way. She had her baby the last week of January. And she didn't look. She never knew whether it was a boy or a girl. They told her it was healthy, and that satisfied her.

16 | It was just sundown when the bus made the Claypitts stop. Before I had a foot on the ground, I saw Mom standing outside the door of The Pull-Off Plaza. My knees were wobbly from the trip and from the sight of her, but I collected my suitcase and headed right up there. I figured she wouldn't skin me alive in plain view of witnesses. She didn't.

"Well, Mom, I'm back." Nervous as I was, I was still proud I'd done it.

"You all right?"

"Sure."

"Dr. Courtney called me so I was looking for you. He seemed like a real nice person."

"He is, Mom. They all are."

"Well, how were things up there?"

"You mean Ellen, Mom?"

"Yes. Ellen."

"She's a little confused now, but I think she'll be all right. I think we'll get her back."

"Well, if we do, it's you that saw to it. I couldn't have managed it. I wanted to do something myself, but I didn't know how."

The she turned around quick like she just remembered she had to rush back in to work. "Leave your suitcase here. I'll bring it along after work. You better scoot on home. Liz is anxious to see you."

I started to go, but she said, "It's a mystery to

me where you found the money to make the trip. I don't suppose I'll ever know, will I?"

"No, Mom, I don't suppose so." I headed off toward town then, feeling like I was just back from a trip around the world. Since it was Sunday night, OKLAHOMA OIL: THE MOTORIST'S BEST FRIEND was closed up. I walked carefully around the zinnia bed, all plowed up now for the winter.

I found Liz at the kitchen table, wearing a sweat shirt that reminded me strongly of one of mine and a pair of Levis that made her look like a half-grown stork. But one thing you can say for Liz, she knows how to welcome a person home. When the kissing and hugging were over, she said, "I thought you wouldn't ever come back, Carol. I thought I was the only one left. I couldn't sleep in our room. I moved in with Mom."

"Now you knew better than that. You knew I'd come back. I wouldn't pick up and leave you, would I?"

"Well, I didn't know," she said, but she sounded pleased.

"If you moved in on Mom, who roomed with Otis?" The minute the words were out of my mouth, I knew I'd said the wrong thing. Liz plopped down in the chair and started fingering a little white envelope.

"Otis isn't here, Carol."

"You don't mean Mom—"

"No. You know something, Carol? It was like I thought. Mom knew about Otis right along. From the very beginning. On the night you left, she found your note and read it. Then after a while she said, "All right, Liz, you might as well bring that durn cat out of hiding.

156

"But you remember that sore place on his paw? It got a lot worse. Got so Otis couldn't hardly drag around, and it oozed. It was awful how much it oozed. Yesterday morning, Mom said she guessed we'd better take him to the vet so we did. And when we got him in on the examining table, it took Mom and me and a helper to hold Otis down. It hurt him so bad when the vet touched his sore place he spit and hissed and tried to bite all of us. We couldn't hold him. Then the vet said he'd have to have an operation to cut away all the infected part. He said if it was down into the bone, they wouldn't be able to do much for him. We're still waiting to hear. We won't know till tomorrow.

"I'm scared. I've been praying for him, Carol. Is that silly?"

"No."

"Want to see something? A girl in my class, Althea Troutman, got a camera for her birthday. Last week she was trying it out, and she took a picture of me and Otis. Want to see it?" She slipped the photo out of the envelope. It was all smudgy with fingerprints. Liz was holding Otis up next to her cheek, the pair of them staring straight into the camera.

"I want to get me a frame for that, Carol. Dime store has them snapshot-size.

"Carol, what if he dies? I mean if they had to take his paw off or something, we could manage. I could look after a three-legged cat, but, Carol, what if he dies?"

"Otis is pretty tough, isn't he? Might take a lot to finish him off."

"That's right," she said. "He's real tough."

"Let's just hold on till we hear from the vet,"

I told her. "We'll get together after school to-morrow and go downtown and buy the best frame they've got. I didn't spend all my money on the trip. Just put the picture away till then. It won't hurt so much, Liz. It won't hurt if you don't look."

RICHARD PECK was born in Decatur, Illinois. He attended Exeter University in England and graduated from DePauw University and Southern Illinois University. He has taught at Hunter College High School in New York and has recently served as the Assistant Director of the Council for Basic Education in Washington, D.C. He has published four anthologies of writing for young people: two collections of contemporary poetry and two of non-fiction. More recently, his poetry has appeared in SATURDAY REVIEW. His articles on schools and students have appeared in such periodicals as PARENTS, PTA MAGAZINE, and CHRISTIAN SCIENCE MONITOR.